BABRUI
The Unheard Song of a Warrior

NEEL KAMAL

BlueRose
Publishers
NewDelhi • London

First Published in September 2021

ISBN: 978-93-5472-360-5

BLUEROSE PUBLISHERS
www.bluerosepublishers.com
info@bluerosepublishers.com
+91 8882 898 898

Cover Design:
Cover page Copyright@The Khronos Group Inc.: Neel kamal

Typographic Design:
Namrata Saini

Distributed by: BlueRose, Amazon, Flipkart, Shopclues

AUTHOR BIO

Neel is a banker by profession, a flutist, a painter and a staunch believer in individuality. His parent's professional love for painting, reading and music has given Neel, the most relishing experience by finding love and God in Words, Music and Painting. His first book *My Souls Whisper of Genre Poetry*, revelled with philosophical insight and artistic inclination covering the various subjects of life.

Neel presently lives in Hyderabad happily with his wife Preetisha Krotha.

Connect with Author

www.authorneel.com

www.facebook.com/authorneel90

www.instagram.com/neel11author

www.twitter.com/neel_kamal_90

To Vennela

My dear sister,

a true admirer of Art who

exercised her every power as a sister

to bring the best in me.

Om Namah Shivaya!
Om Namo Bhagavate Rudraya!
submitting my meagre knowledge and
words in totality unto you.

ACKNOWLEDGEMENTS

To my father *Mahesh* and mother *Rani*

Whose nurture has taught me inquisitive values.
To my wife *Preetisha*

who played a major part in
transforming my passion towards a global audience.

I must pass my gratitude to my mother-in-law, *Lalita Karasi*

for she had shown personnel interest in editing the
document.

NARRATIVE STRUCTURE

Babruvahana is a mystical character from the times of Mahabharat. I have tried to bring that character into light, who I felt was a force that will inspire the very core of being. Most of the story is conducted by the use of *Soliloquy* narration which allows the readers to think from the character's perspective. The general storyline takes the style of *parallel narrative* linked by a common theme. The symbol that was used to divide each part of the story is *Sahasra Chakra*.

The most prized part that you already gave me is: your time. I thank you for choosing this book by investing your time in it. You will thoroughly enjoy the reading. This book will take you on a journey of war, love, meditation, besotted art, friendship, and mystified revelations of truth.

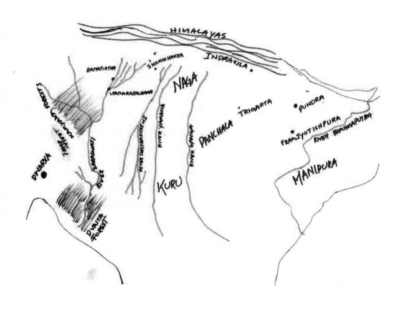

HIMALAYAS

INDRAKILA

RAMATIRTHA

SHARMISHAKRA

VARARAPALINAM

NAGA

PANCHALA TRIGARTA

PUNDRA

PRAGJYOTISHPURA

RIVER BRAHMAPUTRA

FORESTS

GANDHAVA

VIRATA NEAR

SARASWATI RIVER

RIVER DRISHADVATHI

RIVER YAMUNA

RIVER GANGA

MANIPURA

DWARKA

KURU

DWAITA
FOREST

1

CHAPTER 1

Pundra, The cursed battleground—

The dribbling wind fleeting through my rigged skin, blurring my vision for a fragile duration. Perspiring, breathing heavily in a smothered hiss, exhausted sharp-naked eyes in constant lookout for any movement that enemies could make. Seated with one left knee, my right hand held over my heavy sword, finding it arduous to resist the sunlight reflecting from the sharp sword-blade, for it might alert the enemies of our precise position. Sweat dripped in a slow, panicking movement from the forehead, and I waited with the patience of a nine-month womb-carrying mother. I waited with the patience of a forest-dwelling wild animal hunting its prey.

One minor blunder, one slight misadventure, and a misjudgement can prove unsympathetically fatal to the entire army of soldiers, one lakh ninety-eight thousand in total, on a wait like a composed predator, not eliciting a tiniest sound, even with their shallow breaths. They had vigorously trained for the arrival of this blood-filled day. Along with their day-to-day routine of weapon training, they were disciplined at managing frugal meals for day's altogether. This harsh discipline forged the men into solid and sturdy warriors. Today, the day of the Judgement, the day that decides their fate of living or not, the day that determines whether to make their bed with their wives or not. The day that will decide to play, chase, and cherish their cute, bubbly, smiley children or not.

In that agonizing wait, my thoughts were myriad and reoccurring, unable to maintain the pace and chaos. They wandered decades back in time to my home. The land of green paddy blades of grass where I used to play, run, and perform all kinds of mischievous antics along with my friends. In those times, the playfulness that I exerted had a potent and fascinating effect in shaping my consciousness and attitude to the general mysterious workings of nature, which ended with me developing a deep love for nature. I remember it as it was yesterday, the massive tree with a stem so solid and rigid, as large as an elephant's trunk, seated in silence in a quiet east corner of the land, acted as our common resting place, a place for us to indulge in all kinds of chores to pass our time. In the early mornings, before the first daylight, my caring mother would throw tantrums at my laziness, awakening me from my deep slumber. Well, to be frank, I would be up before her ministrations, as the thought of my mother waking me up hits my consciousness and I keep on waiting with my eyes closed, waiting for her to shout, nag, push, and throw me off my sleep. I would finish all my morning chores well before sunrise and hurry myself to reach *Gurudev Lespakamanya*.

My Gurudev, the most skilled warrior Brahmin, devoted all his energies to the all-pervading Lord Shiva. There was a long believed rumour by the villagers that Gurudev, without uttering a word or mantra, deep-seated in Padmasana embraced in silence, can pass an instant-kill to anyone coming under a radius of one hundred and eighty feet. Many believed that Gurudeva acquired the power to generate a seamless radiating deadly effect through prahars (three hours) and days of meditation that would eventually lay down many bodies to smear dust without laying a finger on them but neither have I ever seen Gurudeva perform such a deadly radiating effect nor I wished to see one.

My mother always reminded me that I am blessed to acquire such a teacher for my initial stages of learning. I managed to reach Gurudeva's ashram well before the first light. I washed my feet clean and consumed a Tulasi leaf, as was the custom in the Ashram. I humbly touched Gurudev's feet, who was in deep meditation, turning rudraksha beads one after another in a slow-moving manner. With each deep breath, which once I counted coming around one hundred and eight eye twinkling's, compared with eighteen of mine. He explained the correlation of breath with various factors of life such as fear, anxiety, happiness, and peacefulness during one time. He said, with his eyes half shut, hands clipped in Gyan mudra, "The *uchavasana* (inhalation) and *uchavasita* (exhalation), during the emotions of fear and anxiety, will only take a few eye-twinkling's of time. And, when a conscientious individual creates more equilibrium between uchavasana and uchavasita, involving deeper breaths of larger intervals, one will reach the state of peace and tranquillity."

I silently seated myself next to *Rasikri*, daughter of a shudra who, along with me, was under the tutelage of Gurudeva. Curiously, I had enquired with my mother about why Gurudeva was offering his teachings to a girl who is not only impoverished but also happened to be a shudra. My mother responded by smiling tenderly and said, "Babru, though shudras are considered untouchables by the society, a girl is always treated as an object of desire, restricted only to the corners of household's duties, and fulfilling husband's Dharma. However, Gurudeva never considered male and female as two different entities but two forms of the same divine energy. And as far as the system of caste or division of society is considered, Gurudeva considers Lord Shiva as his godly mentor, Lord Shiva as his way of life. The Lord himself is a caste-less, seamless-energy embracing none and everyone. So, Babru, society's notions are very bewildered and, if taken to be accurate and believed as a way of life, they will lead to utter chaos resulting in becoming a victim of the cycle of birth and death. Hence, to be a man of awareness and of divine nature, give due respect to living and non-living, nature and its elements, you, and me, a shudra and a Brahmin. Every single aspect of this chaotic universe is different forms of energy and energy alone. Never try giving it neither a shape nor an identity. Then and only then, will you be reaching the highest levels of understanding, without travelling to the farthest lands. By being in one place, you will be enlightened."

With these thoughts running in my mind, I looked and greeted Rasikri a pleasant good morning with a cherishing smile. She reverted with a smile of tiny, stretched lips, making a small pit in her cheeks with her eyes extended to their respective ends and her hands turning upside revolving cutely down. *O, God, I just love witnessing her bubbly smiles, compelling me many times to invent humour, to impress and witness her smile.* We both resumed the Padmasana (Erect seating position with crossed legs) with rhythmic breathing in long moments of waiting for Gurudev to open his eyes. In the initial days of tutelage, I was very impatient to wait and reluctant to learn, but..........

My horde of thoughts was interrupted by the sudden voice of my second-in-command, *Durvasana*, asking for my permission to engage highly trained twenty one thousand, seven hundred and four archers to shoot at enemies. The enemies were maintaining low visibility with only some heads moving here and there, six hundred meters away from us. And Durvasana cannot be blamed for his judgment to attack. My silence to his request with no instant reply is quietly irking the few soldiers who are witnessing the exchange, and I can clearly understand their impatience, for they want to finish the battle, go home and have plenty of wine and relax. But my silence cannot be misconstrued as my weakness or unpreparedness as I was trying to comprehend the battle psychology of the most feared army we have ever had faced. Many questions occurred in my head. *Why were they, after a prahar (three hours) of silent waiting, displaying their heads in an odd position? Few in the left flank and few in the right. Are they expecting us to attack? What if we attack? We might expose our carefully formed battle position to the enemy.* And suddenly, I remembered Gurudeva's words about battle, "Battle is not about numbers and skills alone, it's about patience and perceptive capability to understand the enemies. To acquire a dominating position in the war, first and foremost, we need to weaken their sturdy minds and tough psyche. Keeping that in mind, battle formations and positions should be planned."

Keeping my eyes glued to the enemy's position, I gently raised my hand, pointing at Durvasana, commanding him to wait for my instructions. I needed to manage the growing anxiety, spreading like a wildfire amongst the soldiers and had to contemplate the wild goose strategy the enemies might be discussing. I asked my battle advisor and closest friend, *Suprasena*, about his plan of action and the available options. Suprasena replied, "My prince, we cannot possibly risk more loitering as this might infuriate many anxious soldiers into acting wildly, resulting in the entire battle turning in favour of the enemies. So, we need to strategize the attack as early as possible."

I looked at Suprasena in an irritated fashion and admonished him lightly, "Stop addressing me as prince, Suprasena." *I know he will never adhere to this but I hated being called prince, 'Prince of the powerful', 'Super prince', 'Universal prince', 'God of princes', and other glamorous names the court poets invented to address me.* I looked at

Suprasena with a sly smile and he smirked back at me. *Suprasena had been my dearest companion since the past, I don't remember, like eleven or twelve years.*

I was in my mid-twenties when my grandfather was ruling the kingdom. At that time, I was indulging in my whims and unbothered about the consequences. I used to create quite a ruckus in the neighbourhood by riding my wild white horse-like with an enchanting madness. Its loud and noisy whinnies at ungodly hours, sure gave many, a troubled night's sleep. And amongst the disturbed ones was Suprasena. His oval rounded face provided space for a mildly sharp nose and the wild set of eyes gave the impression that he was a glutton, bookish and more of a gentle rule monger. Noticing my troublesome behaviour, the five feet ten-inch glutton, in an angry mood, commanded me to halt. I was surprised and had squinted at the person who had found the audacity to raise his voice and shout at me. It was obvious, either he didn't have knowledge about my lineage, or he was superbly dumb. However, in an aggrieved tone, he yelled at me to halt. I obliged in an indignant manner. Stepping down from my beautiful tiresome horse, *even my horse might be cursing me,* as I made a few circular steps around him, studying his posture, with a devilish face.

However, Suprasena, without a hint of intimidation, delivered a longer than usual monologue about my prided behaviour causing excessive trouble. He went into lengths about goodness, evil, God, a way of life, and the law of karma. I was desperate to retaliate, but felt it was risky and stupid. If I had uttered one more word, and a thousand annoying words were waiting to burst out of Suprasena mouth. I believed escape from this prodigious, annoying individual was the best available alternative and I silently conveyed my apology, ascended the horse, and rode away. I realized the best conscious decision I had ever made was to not retaliate and enter a banter with Suprasena. *For only God knows my sleepless nights had it been otherwise.*

A few days later, I was passing-by the local market, making some purchases and, I found myself staring at a little lesser than an obese figure. He bore a striking resemblance to the man I had an altercation with, a few nights ago. Strangely, he was working in a local tax collection department that my grandfather oversaw personally. The tax department was considered to be the most sensitive area, so I knew my grandfather could not afford even the slightest blunder in this department as it concerns the welfare of the kingdom. Nevertheless, minor wilful tax avoidances and malpractices did occur right under his collar, which cannot be corrected nor traced back to the source. But a close watch and periodic scrutiny would enable proper functioning of the tax department.

Hence, I was shocked as well as perplexed to see the man working in this department. I couldn't contain my curiosity and enquired about the bold, fat person. *The same man who had the innate audacity the previous day to confront and lecture me on the value and life system, something I had never bothered to give the faintest attention to*. So, I stopped by the tax department, and was not surprised to see the amount of intensified work the employees indulged in with a profound dedication.

Sensing my presence, a junior coin-keeper hopped towards me. He was a bit small for his age, had a boxed face with some odd white patches occupying both cheeks. *Looking at him, I realised that I could basically count every bone in his body.* Going by the name of *Pinakini,* he rushed towards me and then escorted me to the luxurious inner chambers that are allowed only to a few members. For it is the most complex and secure house consisting of coins, gold, precious metals, and most important of all – *Tada Patra (palm leaf)* manuscripts to record the lineages, scientific discoveries, poetry, philosophical debates, and battles containing detailed strategies. On my arrival, I was graced with coconut water and barberry fruits. *Well, the cultivation of barberry fruits has a long history. The fruit owes its origin to the land of Yavaniens, who gifted us with the seeds of barberry fruit some decades ago.* Pinakini, all excited and exuberated, humbly asked me of my good reasons for passing by the tax department. I grinned at him and showered him with some unintended praises as I enquired about the total assets and liabilities of the kingdom, and then slowly propelled towards the health and welfare of the employees. While he was bragging about each employee in detail, *which is of no interest to me,* I listened patiently, and stopped him mid-way when he threw light on the fat and cheeky human being. Pinakini uttered with a smirk, "His name is Suprasena."

So, Suprasena it is, I muttered inside of my mind. However, Pinakini could not stop himself from praising Suprasena. I listened to him with all the fortitude, as he continued and on about Suprasena's intelligence, conduct, work ethics, and strict adherence to work timings.

Suprasena was also bestowed with a few silver coins and a stamped manuscript from my grandfather, *Chitrasena*, acknowledging his contribution to eliminating starvation in the kingdom with his exemplary study and research on "Improvement in the Crop Production." My animosity gave way to curiosity as I discovered more about his way of life. I couldn't help but accept that I was greatly impressed with his accomplishments. One of which was to be in the good books of my grandfather, and I considered that to be a miraculous feat. My growing hunger to learn more about him compelled me to request Pinakini to get him acquainted with Suprasena, which he readily obliged but had a shocked, dubious look on his short and crushed face. Pinakini accompanied Suprasena and brought him to my chambers. *O' the trembling tummy carrying his oval head. May God forbid my amusing thoughts.*

When Suprasena entered the chambers, he found himself shocked and outraged by my presence there. He threw a stern look at Pinakini and reprimanded him for allowing me to enter the sacrosanct place. Pinakini tried to explain my lineage to him. However, he showed no signs of calming down. I understood the reason for his displeasure and quickly asked for his forgiveness for the ruckus I had caused the previous night. His bulky chin nodded slowly and graciously accepted my apology.

11

I must admit, he had a charismatic charm. Without his intelligence and his thought process, I would have never sought to seek forgiveness from him. After that brief encounter, we spent a lot of time discussing philosophical ideologies, debating ancient scriptures, playing games and riding horses. In a way, he played a vital role in harnessing my conscience, and I, in return, taught him defence tactics and warfare, swordplay. Our initial misconstrued hatred turned into a good friendship.

Once, during *Malyudh—* (*head-on-head combat that involved strength and technique and was played typically on clay surface with the framed rules, one shouldn't hit below abdomen level. Victory will only ensue when the opposite party surrenders*), there were four teams of eight members each. The winner was to take home three horses belonging to each of the losing teams. Suprasena wasn't playing but came out to cheer and support our team, which by the way, was on the verge of winning at the end of round five. But, during the final round, when I entered the ground to combat, I heard the only word that I always wished and prayed to never hear. A word that drenches my soul into fragility and robs my senses entirely into a complete black-out. The opposing team and their supporters started screaming, "Bastard son" repeatedly. It seemed obvious that they intended to demoralize me and take control over the losing game. That firm and sturdy resonance echoed inside my mind, and my senses lost sanity into condensing my body into a numb state. Witnessing the materialization of events, Suprasena, without batting an eye, rescued and dragged me to a resting place amidst the horrendous noises and vile laughs running wildly through the air. He splashed some water on my face until I regained control. Moments after, I spectated the most aggrieved and unseen avatar of Suprasena. His raging eyes, sheer madness in his high-pitched cry, his chest-thumping and enraged breathing sent waves of terror across the on-lookers. He marched like a wounded elephant towards the intimidating team. Grabbing a four feet Gadha (a Wooden Mace) lying glued to the soil, he jumped high into the group of opposing team and the weapon released swiftly into the right arm of the first point-of-contact. The wounded person wailed loudly, "Amma... Amma (Mother......, Mo...ther)", having his right shoulder tilted down, dislocating his shoulder bone. The act frightened and trembled the other group members into chaos and confusion and many managed to run away from the sheer defiance that Suprasena unleashed.

Nevertheless, some stood their ground and arose to fight Suprasena. Without a moment's hesitation, with neither a thought nor technique, Suprasena ran right into the bulky wrestler, who was smashing his own thighs inviting him to attack. Suprasena swung the mace at his stomach, which was craftily evaded with the right-leg stepping backward in a swift second. In that split moment, the time required to fetch back the mace allowed the opponents to grab and throw punches at Suprasena. However, even the bullies found it difficult to bring down the hefty and inflated Suprasena to ground. I helplessly witnessed Suprasena being beaten to a pulp by six foes over and over. However, my teammates, who were standing on the side-lines, seeing this commotion, suddenly transformed into aggressive animals, outnumbering the bullies and forcing them to flee for their lives. The assault on Suprasena left him with many minor injuries, requiring him to get bed rest for fourteen-days. *God only knows what became of the guy whose shoulder went haywire with the mace blow. I seem not to recall the exact moment when the angelic convergence manifested between us, but it did happen. When I was in trouble or the whole of humanity had deserted me, I knew for certain that I would have Suprasena's belly to play and tickle with. And I am unmistakably positive that he would never quit on me. My soulful companion for life. I consider myself a lucky man having fate bringing our two energies together. If not for him, my conscience would have been.............................*

The sudden paced exuding sound touched, passed my ears, and brought my dwelling-past to a racing halt. The incessant resonance in the calm whirlwind, and the steel sounds of shields, I can only presume that the enemies wore thin of their patience, and the appearing burst of wheezing sound is that of arrows, coming right at us. Impulsively, I shouted at my most proximate flank to take cover from the impounding arrows. And the Brownish, Serpent-shaped shields, which had an imprint of a *Nandi*— *gate guardian deity of Lord Shiva*, were all raised at once in unison to prevent the oncoming arrows. Some arrows did manage to reach our side but were deflected from our strong raised shields leaving no one gravely injured. Many of the arrows couldn't even penetrate our army camp.

I safely speculated that since this is the enemy's first flight of arrows, they are probably making some wild calculations of the approximate distance between the opposing armies. However, we received an added advantage from observing the flight of arrows. The enemy's position now had been compromised.

Durvasana and I exchanged a rough, canny half-smile, and I assumed our quiet stare had conveyed my orders to Durvasana. Durvasana was six and a half feet tall, three hundred- and eighty-pound hulk, and a man who could instil fear and terror in the eyes of onlookers. He had a strong muscular build with a hard rectangular wolfish-face, sunken wide protruding eyes of brown copper colour. One left thick unruly eyebrow cut halfway during a dreadful ferocious war that Durvasana always boasts of, when he is grossly intoxicated.

Durvasana, having understood my order, responded immediately by quickly making out the distance and the point of origin of the arrows. He then made some hand gestures at the archers, who were under his watch and command. The archers comprehended the orders and quickly arranged themselves in a linear order, dividing themselves into forty-eight rows. Each row had maintained a one yard distance between them, and the soldiers had raised their bows upward, stretching the strings with the three fingers curled, lightly touching the feathers. Durvasana silently ordered them to point their sharp-edge of the arrow at the sky on a seventy-degree angle and then gestured for them to halt. He then held his left hand high to his head with a closed fist, staring at the enemy frontline, waiting for the right moment to pass the order of release.

I silently watched the enemy, who appeared to be reloading the arrows for another round of attack. Over here, a composed Durvasana was waiting patiently for the right moment, to pass his own order of attack.

When the wind slowed down, and the clouds concealed the blaring Sun, leaving only a few rays to protrude out, Durvasana's fist slowly opened and he shouted "Release", signalling his twenty one thousand seven hundred and four archers to rain the terror of arrows at the lurking enemies.

We watched the arrows fly high. Our heartbeats dragged low, bidding those moments time, expecting Durvasana's expertise on distance and angle to be accurate. The arrows landed like heavy thunders as expected and pierced through the front-line soldiers, mostly the infantry, instantly killing many.

The cries and wails were so loud that we could only imagine the damage the arrows had made - *piercing the eyes, digging the lungs, deep trenches in thighs*. But, our first arrow attack was far from being a success. We quickly presumed how our enemies would plan the next assault. They cannot be taken for granted, for they had the vicious history of diminishing and shrinking many affluent and well equipped militaries of smaller kingdoms to ashes.

CHAPTER 2

Dwarka, 3155 BC

"Abhi, that's enough for today," reprimanded *Balarama* with a fuming gaze plastered on his hard-rigged, honey-coloured skin. There were half-moon-shaped heavy wrinkles forged on his face— not due to age but as a consequence of hard physical work accumulated overtime from tilling the farmland that Balarama much of the time indulges in by himself.

"I have specifically instructed you to perform only six sets each consisting of forty to forty-five dands equalling two-forty to two-fifty dands (Indian push-ups). But, your persistent stubbornness in not adhering to my instructions has become repetitive, and you keep on overdoing the dands, sometimes totalling four hundred and eighty. This is abnormal for a six-year-old like you."

With his innocent fish eyes, *Abhimanyu* stared at his uncle with cold feet, mid-way a full dand, two hands lifting the entire flexed body in ninety degrees. Balarama, noticing the mischievous demeanour he undoubtedly acquired from Krishna, hesitantly murmured at Abhimanyu to continue with the dands.

After Balarama reached home, *Subhadra* surged towards him with a glass full of cinnamon water and waited for her brother to settle down. Exceedingly curious, she started to enquire about Abhimanyu's progress in training.

Balarama grabbed Subhadra by her hand with a concerned look etched on his face and gently pulled her to be seated next to him. He lifted Subhadra's chin upward and said, "Sister, I am beginning to worry about Abhimanyu's enthusiastic persona and the possible repercussions it may have in his future."

With her heartbeat humming faster, Subhadra, perplexed and worried, probed further "What might be the reason, brother? Is he not conducting properly? Or is his intellect underdeveloped compared to the pupils of his age or is he not fit to learn about the war-fare?"

"Na, Subhadra, your questions stand no relevance at all. I am deeply worried because Abhi is far more intelligent and competent than an average adult. His gripping power, along with his gifted memory has made him master every Vedic word with perfect pronunciation. If you listen to his four-minute breathless rendition of a few verses of Aitareya Upanishad, you would be spell-bound. His physical strength too is unparalleled for a six-year-old kid." replied Balarama.

Pradyumna was deeply engrossed in putting down his thoughts onto the manuscript — devising and improvising distinct new battle formations. He looked at his uncle Balarama and stood up to greet him and said, "You must witness the marvel, dear Aunt, our little Abhi weaves with the sword as if Lord Natarajan himself has descended onto Earth immersed in a cosmic dance. The way Abhi has the intriguing notch for learning any kind of art, let it be warrior form of art, dance or acquiring knowledge, we can easily presume that he has the blessings of Lord Karthikeya— the warrior son of Lord Shiva. I am extremely sure that our Abhi will be counted amongst the greatest warriors the Bharatkanda has ever flowered. He will be spoken highly of in resemblance to various warrior gods."

Exhilarated, elated and unable to control the jubilation, Subhadra shed a few tears of glee and mildly told Balarama, "Brother, after listening to what you and Pradyumna had to say about Abhimanyu, I feel I have fulfilled by duty as a mother. Of all the men, you perfectly knew well how challenging it is for a woman to be greeted and respected in a society without her fair share of discrimination. The reason for my distraught was being one of many wives to glorious Arjuna......" scouring the tears with the saree, Subhadra continued, "...the scornful way the people stare at me. Those sarcastic greetings they shower upon me. Those disdainful comments they pass about me, while I am gone. Hugh! They were relishing my helplessness. Whenever my unsettling mind revisits those moments, my soul crushes itself into utter shame. Of course, it is easier for brother Krishna to preach - *every event is a karmic cycle that is eternal but to experience various forms of jeering discriminations is impalpable*. But whenever I pose a question to brother Krishna about why men are treated as heroic when they have multiple wives and women subjected to ridicule, they are of those wives? He always responds to me with that teasing smile in the end, ending with a karmic explanation. Some brave people even dared to question Arjuna's whereabouts for the past five years? As to why am I staying in my parental home? Did he go to pay visits to other wives? Such disgusting questions I am compelled to face. Why? All because I was born a woman. Such a noble and sane society that we so carefully created and are incredibly proud of. And brother, today, yours and Pradyumna's words have confirmed that my life's dharma is on the right path. But, please enlighten me, brother, what is it that is gravely bothering you about Abhimanyu?"

With a deep contemplative sigh and outrageous voicing, Balarama said, "Subhadra, whenever I get to hear the sheer stupidity of ignorance, the evils of society have inflicted on you and all the women. You have no idea how much my blood fumes into vicious eruption, and how I wish I could punch those idiotic person responsible to death just using my bare fist. But, you never intend to reveal the identity of the persons responsible as you always feel that the mental incapacity is a far larger evil than the individual insanity that has crept into our society. You also say that practises cannot be subdued with violence but with awareness and comprehension alone. I cannot help but agree with you on this. Your nightmare of experiences has opened our blind eyes to the harsh realities and the torment that our women have to endure. Keeping that as a priority, as you are well aware, we had passed an ordinance making it a punishable offense of rigorous two-year imprisonment for whomsoever indulged in indecency, improper treatment, sexual harassment and domestic violence against women. Thanks to you and *Rukmini*, who have contributed constructively to drafting the particulars of this law. I must particularly laud the intuitive suggestions that Pradyumna offered and we have successfully implemented. The fruits of his suggestion bore the results albeit years later. His various suggestions such as offering regular brain-storming jobs to women or involving them in teaching, education, or participation of women in local body elections. Those suggestions played a spectacular influence in changing people's consciousness at large and in reducing gender disparities thereby giving equal rights to women."

Pradyumna and Subhadra thanked Balarama wholeheartedly, Balarama continued, "Coming to Abhimanyu, I must reinforce, he is an excellent kid for his age unparalleled to none. His physical strength, his willingness to near perfection of any art form as Pradyumna rightly said, will draw attention of both, the wicked and the powerful alike. By God's grace, the intensity with which Abhi is thriving and evolving, I can already perceive his skills will be phenomenal as a warrior by the time he reaches thirteen or fourteen years of age."

"Isn't that a good thing to hear, brother?" Subhadra curiously enquired with a small chuckle playing on her charred lips.

Balarama said, "Yes, Subhadra. Indeed, it's a delight for any parent to learn great things about their child. A parent cannot wish for more, beholding Abhimanyu. But, here is where the trouble lies: does the unprecedented ingenuity that Abhimanyu possesses be in any way beneficial to him? I am afraid the answer has to be a plain no."

Pradyumna and Subhadra shot Balarama a shocked expression and asked "Why?" exchanging curious glances with each other.

"Because for one, he adds great strength to the side he is fighting for. During this phase he will become the prime factor both for the Army he is fighting for and the opposing side. Moreover, with the agility with which Abhimanyu is progressing, he will be remembered as one of the greatest warriors this earth has ever given birth to. And moreover, every army would wish to have Abhimanyu fighting on their side. Wouldn't they?"

Realizing the confusion reeling on Pradyumna and Subhadra's faces, Balarama continued, "To put it in simple terms, if supposedly I am the chief commander of an army, I would rely heavily on Abhimanyu's shoulder to completely turn the battle to my advantage. At the same time, if I am in the opposing army, I will try every possible way to eliminate Abhimanyu by hook or by crook, paying no heed to the battle rules promised at the beginning of the war to abide by."

"So, in a way, Abhimanyu will decide the fate of the war." Subhadra said.

"Yes, in all probability." replied Balarama.

"Eventually, the enemies will devise every evil strategy to eliminate Abhimanyu at any cost to save their faces." Rattled at the repercussions of having a genius for a child, Subhadra, with a glimmer of hope, probed further, "Does brother Krishna and my husband know about this?"

"I don't believe Arjuna knows, but Kanha (Other name of Krishna), I believe, has been aware about this since Abhimanyu's very birth. He even tried to stop Arjuna midway while he was teaching entryway tactical manoeuvring in *Chakravyuh battle formation* to infant Abhimanyu." Balarama said.

"Hm.....so brother Krishna did foresee Abhi's unperceivable future with his rare capabilities." uttered Subhadra carrying a deep thought to herself, "But, not teaching the exit strategy of Chakravyuh won't stop triumphant Abhimanyu from entering into Chakravyuh. Rather it will land him in more trouble."

"Witnessing the pace, determination, and tenacity with which Abhi is evolving, we can easily infer he will breach the Chakravyuh even without the knowledge of exit strategy." Pradyumna apprised.

Suddenly little steps could be heard becoming louder and louder with the rapidly evolving pace and all three members turned their heads towards the sound. With a large thudding noise, Abhimanyu barged into the hall and jumped into Pradyumna's arms. He had a large beaming smile on his face as he yelled, "Dada (brother), pinch my biceps and feel the hard muscles. I made four-hundred and eighty-three Dands and one-hundred and eight Surya namaskara's," he proudly declared.

Beholding Abhimanyu's cuteness with a tiny bit of apprehension, everyone grinned delightfully, and Pradyumna tickled and teased him saying, "Indeed, your arms are rock solid. Ouch, my hands do hurt a bit touching your arms. There is no denying that your physical stamina bypasses every powerful living man."

CHAPTER 3

The savages of Himalayan foot—

Our spies spread over many parts of North Bharatkanda, to keep an eye on the enemies we are presently facing. They described the Manikuntekans as the gut-wrenched cannibal's, inhabitants to the trenches of the bushy hills of *Manikunteka*. Located between the rampant busiest cities of Videha and Shravasti, placed approximately one hundred and fifty miles east of river Ganga and one hundred and ninety miles south of Himalayan foot. The Manikunteka hills are not suitable to accustom human settlement.

The local administration of the city of Videha strictly enforced the orders prohibiting their citizens from going anywhere near the vicinity of *Manikunteka* hills.

Once, the young of lovers in their mid-twenties, disregarded the warning and went quite far near the hills to have some private space to themselves. But, as fate would have it, after searching for nearly six days, they were found dead. The dreaded sight of their torn bodies caused a lump in the throats of the citizens. Their eyes were carved-out, bodies covered with teeth marks punched through their hard skin and the whiff of spices evident from the rubbings all over the skin.

The citizens of Videha speculated that both the bodies were first gruesomely destroyed, then assaulted, chopped into pieces, and were dined – *some chewing the bare body and some enjoying the devour along with the spices, etc.*

This horrendous incident sent quivers to the citizen's already petrified minds. Thus, shortly after, Videhan principally elected members in an emergency meeting unanimously declared that crossing the fences is a punishable offense, which no one dared to cross since the horrifying incident.

Manikuntekans were purely driven with the insurmountable appetite to crush, subjugate and physically violate men and inconsolably assault women, regardless of age, creed, or colour. Their inclinations and impulses were so bizarre and utterly disordered that their primal thrust to survive and thrive is driven by a solely unquenchable craving for lust and food.

After careful analysis and inspection of the Manikuntekan's habitat, the devious and trickery master, Radhasaki concocted a deceitful plan to draw the beastly Manikuntekans into his hold. Their disorganized state of animal behaviour, strengths, and weaknesses were closely observed and scrutinized for months together by Radhasaki.

Radhasaki is considered to be a courageous, cunning, spirited, and an intelligent man. Gifted with a cognisant aptitude in military affairs and having excellent proficiency in fencing.

Radhasaki keenly surveyed the behavioural aspects and the incredible muscular strength possessed by the Manikuntekans and introspected the odds of procuring the Manikuntekans into his own enfold by harnessing their skills with reasonable additional discipline and rigorous practice. The deceitful design if executed, he would at last be able to rule and squeeze the substantial kingdoms into conformity. He could even compel the bizarre people on their knees. Radhasaki detests rulers following the rigid structures of administration, emulated blindly from scriptures of Vedas. He lost his only brother to one such kind of ruling. Execution without a fair trial. His fault— *he plundered a wheeled vehicle transporting piles of food to another city and distributed the food to the starving families.* No matter how much Radhasaki tried to reason with the royalty, the death sentence of his brother was not amended. Neither of them was provided with a fair chance to put forward the arguments because they were born into the lowest strata of society. It always pricked him into believing his brother would have been alive, had they taken birth into an upper caste family. Rather than the death sentence, he might have been left with a less, severe punishment.

After the execution of his brother, Radhasaki organised a group of agitated people and trained them. When the time was right, they attacked and gruesomely decapitated the prince's head in the same manner his brother was beheaded. His vengeance didn't stop there. He made it his life's ultimate purpose of eliminating every fascist ruler. Anyone driven by a set of rules, scrapped faith, the practitioner of inequality, the upright supporter of discrimination and upholder of caste system was his target of vengeance.

Radhasaki eternally dreamed of establishing a society where no man will be branded as a sanctified God or a notable dignitary. No person will be engraved as poor or a negligible person. Every available resource will be equally shared, unbiased. Every child born will be the child belonging to the entire community and every individual distress is everyone's crisis. The acquired property as well as the hard work will be equally distributed. No person will be treated with selective discrimination or arbitrary avoidance.

However, for his dream to thrive and see the light, he needed the vital, the most crucial thing, a powerful army at his behest. He travelled to lengths in search of that kind of desired army. When he came across Manikuntekans, he decided he had got one such army. However, to acquire them, Radhasaki's had to earn the trust of Manikuntekans. He had already devised the plan. Flawless execution was the need of the time.

Radhasaki had to spend nine days earning the trust of barbarian's. He conducted a thorough research and soon found out that their weakest link. Something Manikuntekans were most vulnerable to was their unquenching appetite for lust and food. He observed that their essentials were depleting day by day as they had kept themselves restricted to the hilly terrain throughout their lives and never considered migrating to new places.

And all Radhasaki had to do, was find the smartest Manikunteka, engage him in a long dialogue, convince of the potential risks and problems that come with confining oneself to one particular place and promise him the possession of huge lands, a great deal of food and human bodies which will quench their insatiable lust and craving for food. Radhasaki, without a tinge of error, accomplished the planned objective with his manipulative silver tongue. In time, he became the self-proclaimed king of Manikuntekans and the military commander with two lakhs and eighty thousand blood-thirsty beasts under his command ready to kill anyone in a blink of an eye. Now all he needed to do was to train these cannibals into disciplined soldiers.

The soldiers are under a false impression that we are on the verge of winning the war— *no denying that we had a minor advantage with the thumping arrows at Radhasaki's army.* However, the military chiefs and I are positive that the Manikuntekans cannot be taken for granted. Radhasaki had imbibed a well-nurtured and systematic training of sword manoeuvre, skilful arrow targeting, and can endure copious amounts of pain.

Suddenly, we heard a thumping sound which seemed to be coming from the ground. Dust and little rocks were plummeting into thin air and tumbling back down. The sound was becoming unbearable with each passing moment. As anxiety pushed us to imagine the worst-case scenario, we each anticipated an assault by giant elephants and I could see the fear that spread across our flanks.

But it was something else we never thought of, neither the elephants nor any other wild animals, sensing the acceleration of approaching thudding sound. *A giant flock of wild Bulls* numbered in thousands rapidly galloping towards us. They had hugely built bodies with horns the size of its limbs and were covered in a thick coat of fluffy hair. The sight sent chills down our spine. We had miscalculated his intelligence. Radhasaki's counterattack was nothing short of brilliance— leaving tamed wild bulls at us. The damage would be irreparable, leaving behind crushed bodies and decimating the major chunk of the army to oblivion. If we did not strategically counter the attack, our army's strength will be cut in half, compelling us to surrender to their brutality without putting up a brave fight. Beholding the dreaded sight, I immediately ordered every superintendent in charge of their respective flanks into forming a double-wedged crossed formation. Comprehending the orders, infantry, archers, and the cavalry arranged themselves into their respective positions. Infantry dominated the front lines of the "X" shape. Well-built men occupied the first line of the formation carrying bell-shaped shields on both the side-fronts. Left-flanked soldiers were holding the Trishul-shaped (Trident) spears pointing to the east, and the right-flanked soldiers pointing to the west, occupied the rest of seven rows.

The thumping sound was growing louder and noisier with each passing moment, with the Bulls ferociously steering nearer and nearer. When the fierce beasts were only a hundred meters away, we were taken aback by an attack of arrows landing right upon us. All this while, we were planning to deflect the bulls, but we somehow forgot to take the arrows in account. The impounding arrows in the air enveloped the radiant blue sky, concealing the swollen Sun, setting the darkest night for a pint of moments over us.

The three front rows of infantry held their respective shields to the ground, focusing primarily on the approaching wild bulls. They were completely taken by surprise when the unexpected rain of arrows showered upon them. Confusion steered into their minds leaving them less time to react. The arrows pounced upon, piercing our men, chopping off their ears and eyes into halves. The metallic brass helmet was not able to withhold the sharp arrows, leading the edged arrows directly to the heads, resulting in many deaths. The bulls were no exception, receiving a wide pillage of arrows that stitched to their thick-hided skin causing no major damage to them. The wedge position forged to deflect the bulls soon became vulnerable to be breached.

Ashvadhyakshas (Archers), Rathadhyakshas (Cavalry), and I took cover under the shields. Few of the unguarded horses took the tumultuous hit and were killed along with many men. I was shell-shocked to see many of my brothers and friends falling to the ground dead, draped in thick red blood. Despite the fatalities, the soldiers held the wedge formation "X" intact. They successfully managed to deflect the raging bulls by locking and releasing them to run-for in a southward direction by providing a tiny opening at the point of contact between the two opposite parallels of Wedge "X." *We had just avoided a frightful horror.*

Three sharp-edged arrows had managed to dig a hole and pierce through my shield. *Jubi Chacha*, the most trusted aide of our kingdom, had designed my shield. He specializes in the field of chemicals and metals. Rendering us with his valuable services for forty-eight years, he had specially designed my serpent-shaped shield with iron-carbon alloy, inducing it impenetrable by any steel or iron. So, when the arrows found their way into the shield, it bewildered me. I surveyed the arrow for a moment, and realised that the arrow-head or tip was a simple stone with the shaft, being light-weighted wood. I perceived the shock in Suprasena's face, who happened to be scrutinizing the arrow for a while. And Suprasena slackly grinned, "Simple yet brilliant piece of mind." He then further went on to explain the science behind the arrows, "The sharpening of the tip of stone takes a lot of forbearance making the arrow fly in relativity to the wind to the desired destination. And when the arrow reaches its full length, preparing itself to fall onto the earth, it will gather five times more velocity than the steel tip as the weight of the stone exceeds that of steel, propelled with their lightweight wooden shaft." I now realized why the arrow had been able to pierce my iron-carbon shield. *Velocity and weight.*

Witnessing the horrendous bloodbath and seeing the splattered body parts of my fellow soldiers spread over the battleground shook me to my nerves, provoking my deep trenched tears and intimidating my senses to unbearable torment.

Numerous questions crossed my troubled mind. *How would I answer their children? How would I be able to face the wailing women? Even if we managed to win the war, will any of this matter without my fellow soldiers by my side? I cannot again experience the smiles, the jest, and the funny banter we have had. What purpose does the war serve? Are we fighting for the right cause to serve the right purpose?* Noticing my turmoil and momentary apprehension that was driving me to numbness and stupor, Suprasena gazed at me with empathy, throwing a punch to my shoulders, he said, "We are not fighting a war to conquer lands and accumulate riches, my prince. We are defending the helpless innocents back home who will be at greater risk from the encroaching barbarians."

Listening to his admonition, I instantly regained my strength and took a deep breath to calm my senses down. I let out a deep breath-out to expel all the unfavourable thoughts out of my body and mind. Even amid this frightening bloodbath, I wondered to myself that *Suprasena could not address me with my name like he used to do, such a Dumbo.* Then I looked at my army with a stern look and then turned my gaze towards the enemy lane. I observed the sun nearly turning into a giant red ball, implying we had about two hours for twilight to set in and the day one of the war would come to a close.

I instructed Suprasena to set out and organize two groups of four people each— agile, quick on feet, and sharp eye-sighted. The groups must be sent in the directions of enemies, discreetly, avoiding enemy-line contact and return once they have discovered where Radhasaki was concealing the food essentials. Suprasena carried out the order with a smirking grin as he was asked to, sending his eight best men to complete the task without fail. He chose short men as he thought men of this stature would move as quiet as a mouse and finish the assigned task without risking suspicion.

CHAPTER 4

The wilderness of Kamyaka forests and the Exile, 3152 BC

Seated in Padmasana, on top of a large oval rock that dissects the calm flowing Trinavindu Lake, immersed in Kriya yoga with his closed eyes, Arjuna sat chanting "Om Namah Shivaya" for second prahar straight but was finding it difficult to escape from the thoughts of his son Abhimanyu.

It had been nearly nine years since he had promised Subhadra that he would return to Abhimanyu in one year. However, that promise has not been fulfilled and has been prickling Arjuna ever since. The thought of him grown-up, the charismatic beauty he carries, the strength he emulates, every tiny detail was left to fair imagination from the various narratives Krishna offers on his occasional visit to the forest.

With a deep inhalation felt to the guts, the six-foot strong athletic build, the mid-sized beard forming on the soft cheeks, hair knotted on top with a sharp wood, the pleasantly personable Arjuna opened his eyes, stood up and washed his hands clean. He paid obeisance to Lord Shiva, and commenced walking towards the Griha, a temporary shelter built to accommodate the Pandavas and Panchali. The daily Kriya (practice) had become a routine for Arjuna. He engaged himself in meditation with absolute solitude and calmness, as advised by grand teacher Sage Vyasa who frequented his visits to the notched shelter.

However, the shelter which was created with the active help of forest dwellers came at a high cost. The second eldest of the Pandavas, Bheema had to kill the powerful demon king of the forest, *Hidimb*. This was only possible with the motivated help of the demoness of the forest, *Hidimbi*. She is the sister of Hidimb. All this was feasible due to the enchanting allurement Bheema had on Hidimbi. When Hidimb learned about the settlement of Pandavas in his forest vicinity, he quickly ordered his sister, Hidimbi, the most dreaded sorceress, to eliminate the Pandavas. Nevertheless, the Gods had different plans for her. When Hidimbi came in proximity to the seven-foot overly handsome Pandava, she was transfixed at the sight of him. She stared in awe at the graceful beauty. Broad bow-shaped shoulders roped with heavy muscles, rock strong thighs as sweat dripped from the nape of his neck to the muscled back. His eyebrows twirled upward at mid-section and he had a sharp nose, loosened four-foot abundant curly-haired, blooming handsome man swept her heart. One of her entourage informed her that the giant chopping down the massive trees was none other than Bheem. She dropped her jaw in flabbergast. For a moment, she was lost in thought, *is this the person I came out here to execute? He certainly doesn't look like a human being but an angel lost his way in the heaven, finally settling on the earth.* Hidimbi could not stop herself from staring through the little space created from a few layers of leaves at Bheem's deltoid and spinal muscles which curved due to continuous splashing of the heavy metallic sword onto the mammoth trunk of the tree that only a few can flexibly carry. In that very moment, she realized that the silence that echoed, bloomed and reverberated through her entire sentient nerves was nothing but her deep adulation and love for Bheem.

CHAPTER 5

The rain of malignant poison—

It was the right time for the deployment of the castor-bean arrows. I instructed Durvasana to organize the archers in the formation of a triangle. Infantry guarding the outer layer, followed by the archers.

As instructed, Durvasana, with his eyes blazing red from vengefulness, took a deep breath and carried out the triangular formation in a jiffy. His forty-one-inch chest rose high and he gestured forward with his hand pointing at the enemy line at a certain angle. Deciphering the order and the angle of arrows, the Ashvadhyaksha's drew the arrows from a separate quiver that had a pointed blade as the head rather than the usual arrows. They picked a steel box attached to their abdominal region, opened the box cautiously and placed it on the ground. They dipped the arrowhead into the liquid that the box contained. Shutting the box carefully, the box was reverted to their waist. The archers set the arrows in the bow and pulled the bowstring hard. They raised their bows and simultaneously released the arrows when a booming voice commanded, "Release!"

Nineteen thousand men discharged their weapons at Manikuntekans. The flight of the arrows, wrapping the evening sun and battering heavily at the

Manikuntekans. The noise of the arrows hitting against the metal bodysuits could be heard. Many soldiers died instantly as the arrows pierced their hearts and skulls. Still, several of the Manikuntekans effortlessly managed to pluck the blade-arrows out of their bodies. They stood tall, screaming with derision, ridiculing us and thumping their chest with lurking pride.

Meanwhile, Durvasana closely scrutinized their bodily movements. He smirked and passed the order of another castor-bean attack. Ashvadhyaksha's executed with one more arrow attack pouncing blade-arrows at the foes. But this time, the enemies riding with the insane pride mocking our arrow ineffectiveness did not even try to protect themselves with the shields from the impounding of the arrows. Every arrow that we released was deflected by Manikuntekans with their weapons, and though some got pierced in their legs, hands, and the chest, they effortlessly removed it and tossed away the arrows.

This allowed them to mock us, louder than before. Durvasana, tapping his fingers at his lips with a mild grin, repeated the order for the castor-bean arrow attack to take place for six more rounds, and we were received with the same anticipated mockery from the Manikuntekans. Even the leader of Manikuntekans, Radhasaki was not able to hold back his smile, realising no major fatalities transpired in his army with the ineffective, powerless arrows. Then, Radhasaki ordered the infantry to proceed for the ground attack.

Manikuntekans were charging at us like possessed beasts, some sprinting voraciously with all the four limbs, while others were jumping like wild cats from the barren ground to the hard rocks emitting loud cries. Nevertheless, we remained motionless and still. Our Patyadhakshas (infantry) formed the defence position and assumed the *Tortoise* formation, carrying long spears clutched between the Shield's edges.

Few nights ago, during the planning hour of the council which consisted of chief commanders, military strategists, war formation experts, Suprasena, and myself, Durvasana presented the idea of altering the battle strategy. It was decided that Durvasana will divide the archers into two groups. One group will use the regular arrows, and the remaining archers will continue with the castor-bean arrow attack.

The men set their left foot back, held their positions keeping a two yard's distance between them, and started hurling the dipped blade-arrows at the foes. The other group of archers in the middle of tortoise formation assaulted the charging infantry with regular arrows.

Nine minutes had passed since the onset of the castor-bean ambush. We were eagerly waiting for the effect of the dipped liquid to recede. And then, we shortly discovered that the running velocity of Manikuntekans was on a continuous decline. Swaying inconsistently in their steps, their limbs unmoving and numb, their lips distorted, and bodies immobile. They had started to topple on the ground irregularly. We looked at their aghast faces and witnessed the horror-filled event. Their eyes were bulging out, with visible red veins, leaking thick mounts of blood. Radhasaki could not understand the afflicted terror that was unleashed. Even we were stunned to helplessness and did nothing but sympathize with the agonizing pain the collapsing soldiers were enduring.

Radhasaki moved towards the forefront and noticed his soldiers were crushed, faceless, and fluttering. His comrades were plunging onto the ground instantaneously lifeless. Some were battling to steady their breath, while others had raw blood dripping down their eyeballs. Witnessing the horrendous event, Radhasaki's eyes smouldered with shock and wrath. His crushed boxed face had astonishment and bewilderment etched on it as he glared into the sky and left a loud outcry.

As the sun half-naked lurked between the mountains and the winds hustled, robbing their breaths away, Radhasaki called back his remaining army and called it a day.

The blaring sun soon gave way to the chirping night, witnessing the mobbed slaughter, its glittering rays blurred and faded away as we drew ourselves back to the camp, calling it a day. We quickly evaluated the casualties by the end of day one and realised we had lost around seventy thousand souls to death, nine thousand soldiers of them had minor injuries, and four thousand soldiers were severely injured. Many of our soldiers recounted that gravely mutilated men had to kill themselves, as the pain was intolerable. The suffering resulted in dislocated bones, limbs, and burnt crust of skin. Suprasena estimated around one-lakh twenty thousand Manikuntekans were exterminated, and fifteen thousand men were left with minor and major injuries.

If it were not for the venomous liquid extracted from the castor-bean plant, we would have been at a loss at the end of the day. Suprasena and I glimpsed and started shifting the casualties to the medical treatment centre which was attended by well-versed court appointed physicians.

CHAPTER 6

The melody of Kamyaka; The consummation, 3152 BC

Fixing her intense gaze on Bheem, Hidimbi decided to marry him at any cost. For the first time in her life, she felt the mounting desire to be a wife and a mother. Though, she understood the implications of disobeying her brother. Probably execution. However, beholding Bheem was the best thing that had ever happened to her.

Quickly contemplating all the possibilities, Hidimbi conceived a plan. And she instructed her small entourage to notify Hidimb that Pandavas had captured her alive and he should hurry to rescue her. Abiding by her order, the small army left for the kingdom. She knows somewhere inside of her that Bheem would defeat her demonic brother. This belief instilled confidence in her and compelled her to hatch and execute this plan.

After the small group of her followers left to notify her brother, Hidimbi squeezed a large gasp of air and quickly transformed her giant, hideous, demonic physical self into a tall, lean, curvature-driven body who had a sharp jaw and moon-shaped supple eyes with sweetly curved rosy lips. Her walk drastically translated from long bent diagonal steps to smoothly ridden tiny movements involving the majority of hip muscles.

Hidimbi knew that looks and tempestuous beauty alone will not be able to flatter the conscientious Bheem. So she used her extrasensory perception; the third person's psyche which was principally exercised to apprehend another person's thought process, a technique that she acquired from rigorous devotion and blessings from Goddess Kali. She quickly perceived that Bheem is kind and generous in his heart. He is highly empathetic, and protective of others by nature. So, Hidimbi decided to play the victim card to strike a long conversation with him.

When the right moment arrived, she intentionally ran into Bheem in a quietly perturbed and upsetting state. Noticing the presence of a youthful woman, Bheem was taken aback for a moment, perceptive of such dazzling elegance standing and panting in front of him. He offered some water to the distressed lady who hastily gulped it and humbly mumbled a 'thank you' as she looked at him. Her shimmering moist eyes unfolded fear, anxiety, and desperation in an attempt to escape or in search of protection.

Bheem, discerning the emotions evident from her face, quickly asked with a stern look, "My dear lady, you look lost in this lonesome dark forest. Forgive my intrusion, but I have to ask what might have been the trouble that compelled and landed a woman of royal nature in the wild forest?"

Biting her lips, looking hitherto in fear, Hidimbi innocently stared into Bheem's eyes for a long moment. Unable to hold back his senses and faltering towards the beholden beauty, Bheem seemed to be lost in her comeliness and was clearly confronting the scintillating reflection of sun rays in her eyes.

Upon realizing the softening moment that Bheem was lost into, elated Hidimbi quickly buzzed, "My lord! My name is Hidimbi, the queen of this jungle and sister to king Hidimb. My brother is a devouring Rakshas who contains neither emotions nor sympathy for other living beings, not even his kingdom subjects. The citizens are ravaging in constant fear of losing their lives and livelihood under my brother's rule. So, many of the elders have pleaded with me to reign over the kingdom. But I vehemently objected and refused. However, if word managed to reach my brother's ears, through some deceitful errands exaggerated rumours, that his sister is actively planning a coup to take control of the kingdom, which is totally untrue. My brother, without bothering to know the truth by having a dialogue with me, will order his guards to eliminate me and also place a huge bounty for whoever brings my head."

"So, fearing the execution, you ran away all by yourself." rebuked Bheem ferociously.

Hidimbi could discern the fumes raging from Bheem's face. With his right hand barely pressing the handle of the hugely built oval weapon of mace expressing disapproval. In that very moment, Hidimbi was drawn emotionally towards Bheem's attitude of innocence, his budding thought of immediate rescue, and emphatic nature towards the helpless.

Uplifting the Gadha (mace) with his left hand and placing it on a small rock by pressing mildly his foot and propping the right hand on his hip, Bheem hollered, "My dear lady! I, Bheem, the son of God Vaayu (wind), brother to Lord Hanuman and a Pandava, solemnly swear that no matter how powerful, demonic and barbarous your brother is, I will sever his prided head and place it in your kingdom in an open display glued on top of his own sword. This will serve as a symbol to eradicate the fear that has seeped into the minds of your citizens. But my actions can only be possible with your positive approval."

Her heart humming with an enchanted beat of exhilaration at the authenticity, clarity, and caring noticeable at Bheem's resonance. Rupturing with ecstasy, Hidimbi replied by saying, "Highness, I bow myself in reverence to your benevolent compassion and readily responsiveness. Let me swear to the Goddess mother Mahakali witnessing the ongoing colloquy. I feel highly blessed to come across a man of exceptional sensibility and indomitable strength. The traits are quite uncommon for a normal living person to possess." Beaming with elation, Hidimbi continued, "Highness, the only condition that I put before you is that before you proceed towards executing my demonic brother, please take my hand in marriage to you. I know this is a lot to ask for, especially from such a remarkable person like you but, what more can a woman expect in her lone transient life. Every trait that a woman finds herself compatible with, let it be strength, caring, empathy. Everything is perceivable in your stature and demeanour. I am also aware that I cannot compel you into marriage with me. But, I plead with you to give it a thought and consider being a husband to my lone-self, a protector to my insecure soul, and a living God to my prayers."

Glittering and glowing at the inconceivable praises unheard of, Bheem placed his hand on Hidimbi's shoulders and said, "Lady, I sense immaculate devoutness in your emotions. I must say, even my beloved Draupadi, who always boasts only about my unmatchable strength has never recognized my inner emotions as you just did and I genuinely wish I could be able to protect you and hold you until my last breath, but as I said, I have already been married and have a beautiful child by the name of *Sutasoma*."

"My lord, I sincerely thank your good-self for even remotely considering marrying me, have you not been married. My happiness and my delving soul knows no limits, knowing that. With the same thought, I would like to assure you that I won't be mindful of being called your other wife. I will be ecstatic if society calls me the wife of mighteous Bheem. I will most certainly be proud to be called that way," Hidimbi jubilantly said.

"I have to admit. Your bright and authentic spirit did pause my breath to the world of tenderness. Dear lady, I, the righteous Bheem, the wielder of mighty Gadha, wish to make you as my venerable wife but only after I put an end to your barbaric brother and free you and the citizens of this kingdom."

CHAPTER 7

Rendezvous with Castor—

Our kingdom, *Manipura* is surrounded from all sides by the Blue Mountains and the natural undistinguished graceful flora. The large mountains paved the way to the splendid plain flat surfaces, rendering us to establish the conducive atmosphere of starting a civilization in coexistence with nature.

Our land was blessed with the presence of water resources from four river basins originating from Eastern, Western, Northern, and Southern directions. The river basins, along with the tactical elevation of the land, eight-hundred meters above the sea level, pivoted the kingdom as the most suitable for agriculture and subsequent livelihood. Heavy rainfall occurs in the kingdom for most of the year. And the summer is mildly hot compared to other southern parts of the Bharatkanda. Agriculture mainly consisted of harvesting rice, tea, black cardamom, and rubber material.

The forests are abundant with trees of oak, pine, and bamboo. Our forefathers, with their apprehensive economic wisdom, realized the traded economic value of rice, tea, black cardamom, rubber, oak tree, pine tree, and bamboo. They decided to reap the benefits by trading the excess production with deficient foreign countries. Thus, the forefathers had arranged for eight teams of a well-learned group of men, referred to as *Rithikas*. The latter excelled in economics, trade and commerce and were tasked to go into far-off lands carrying the samples of the grown products with the sole purpose of engaging in trade and business.

During the mid-winter, when the north-south winds befell, five teams comprising fourteen high esteemed soldiers accompanied two Rithikas and three foreign language translators as they started off to the unknown lands.

One team went by the southern ocean and crossed *Mahalanka*, a land known for possession of huge quantities of gold. From there onwards, they sailed a large ship westwards carrying samples of various commodities such as rice, tea, black cardamom, rubber, oak tree, pine tree, and the bamboo until they reached *Golapindaratna*. The land of immensely valued diamonds which had a prosperous civilisation.

Upon reaching the southern shore in the bright evening under the yellow-reddish blazing sun which appeared larger to the naked eyes than it was back home, Rithikas were received generously by a principal guardian and a group of female care-takers as well as six well-built soldiers. The crackling sounds of the wild animals were audible from the thick forests. There were tremendously large trees that veiled the entire sky leaving little room for the insignificant light to penetrate. These dense forests are home to thousands of different animals and plant species. As they made their way they noticed large serene river bodies, plunging from the razor-edge hill tops. The Rithikas marvelled at the sight as the stunning wilderness left them speechless.

Rithikas described the Golapindan women as ravishingly the most beautiful, alluringly and attractive creatures they had ever witnessed. Sunlight reflected through their luminescent coal-coloured skin. Their dark eye-balls resembled round cat-like eyes, with a yellow flower and a broad green leaf pierced through their crossed hair bun. Their embroidered clothing was carved from the soft skin of domestic animals. The plant layers below their abdomen and the adorned beads hanging by the ears were largely decorated from the ostrich eggshells. The grooming and the fondness towards outfits further reinforced the perception that the Golapindavans are very particular, endearing, and sensitive to the attire that they always carry.

The men were astutely large, muscularly built and were often seen holding up a sharp spear, dangled with a small knee-length loincloth made of animal skin. They were tremendously delighted and overwhelmed with the traded produce that was presented to them— oak tree, pine tree, rubber, tea, and black cardamom. Pleased with the quality of the product, they decided to establish a long binding trade alliance with our kingdom.

Once my Gurudev Lespakamanya had said that the land Golapindaratna draws resemblance to a huge oval-shaped ball, hauling many civilizations together. Until they were split by the potent, pervading waters of the powerful oceans into cropping up, Bharatkanda and

Golapindaratna. He further mentioned that the people belonging to the south of Bharatkanda and Golapindaratna retain a common origin and presumably belonged to the same class of species. So, technically Golapindavans might have been the primal inhabitants of the present-day Bharatkanda.

The other three teams carried vast trade materials. Comprising twenty-one soldiers, four Rithikas, three social experts, and nine translators, crossed land in the westward direction starting from the city. They passed through the cities of Magadha, Vatsa, Panchala, Kuru and further crossed the Sindhu River up to the cities of *Aswaka and Yavana.*

Aswakans showed no signs of interest in our products but Yavaniens displayed a great deal of liking for our materials. Upon the demonstration, Yavaniens were greatly impressed with the viability of the products. They had immediately forged a long-term, mutually agreed five centuries-long trade alliance, signing the Papyrus sheet with a seal.

Our social experts described the Yavanien men as tall, gruesomely handsome, with a large elongated narrow face, thin-straight and pointed nose. They had thick brownish eye-brows leading to curled-hair, and sharp mirrored half-moon eyes tendering the reputation to the Yavanien men of being the Gods of beauty. Moreover, Yavanien women were of no exception, being equally radiant with their shimmering eyes narrowing down to the long and sharp-pointed nose, their supple lips, and heart-shaped facial bone structure elucidating their sublime flawlessness. They also exhibited a great deal of knowledge and expertise in the study of the universe, chemicals, exemplary sculpting, variable art, philosophy, and in the study of animals and plants. The written knowledge was stored in the form of manuscripts in largely built archives. Their lifestyle provided a great deal of insight and was later incorporated into our system of culture.

Their lines of the richness of life dwelled in daily debates, music, constructive criticism, and intellectual conversations. Unlike us, who concentrated the majority of our energy on acquiring lands, gold, and coins. Conceiving it to be the common belief of richness.

For the very artful purposes, Yavaniens had marvellously built a dedicated Andron (building). Our men had written a great deal in their long summarisation admiring the phenomenal edifice of the archive. The Andron is the sole custodian of immensely formulated knowledge, architectural magnificence, cultural interactions and vividly adopted food habits. The practice of polygamy, weapons used in war, their scientific temper, astrological predictions, planetary positions and assorted punishment structures for various crimes were all situated there. To our surprise, their punishments demanded of the guilty to sanitize the city, farm the lands and help with the ailing patients, etc.

When our Rithikas eloquently rendered the presentation about the products, Yavaniens were truly impressed with the multitude of uses and properties that oak and pine trees contained. Their curious nature requested the Rithikas to elaborate. The presentation ironically continued for one more Prahar. Rithikas obliged and explained, "The oak tree is primarily used for the construction of large ships, timber-based buildings, and as a catalyst for enhancement in agricultural production. The chips of oak are best suitable for making wine barrels that enhance the taste of wine. It also exhibits characteristics of diverse medicinal properties in the treatment for dry throat, anal problems, cracks in the skin, cholesterol reduction, and acute diarrhoea." They continued explaining the various uses of pine trees principally utilized for infrastructure of buildings, tea production, and various medicinal properties treating cough, cold, bronchitis, sinus, urinary bladder inflammation, and insufficient urine production. These properties were demonstrated which lead to an extension of their stay.

Extremely pleased with our uniqueness of services and products, Yavaniens privileged us with the seeds of the Castor-Bean plant. They said, "Castor-Bean plant is one of the rarest species to be found in any corner of the world. The leaves of the plant tend to contain an extremely poisonous character. If consumed, the affected living being will be left paralyzed, numb, and possibly dead in a few minutes. Castor-Bean plants are primarily planted in the areas surrounding the entire farming land to specifically act as a defence from the wild animals that scourge on the plantations and create great damage to the farming output."

CHAPTER 8

Kamyaka forest— The acceptance, 3152 BC

Hidimb was gruesomely beheaded by Bheem's bare hands in single combat. The severed head was paraded openly through the entire Kamanyakan settlement to remove the fear and anxieties which were settled in the minds of dwellers. Overjoyed and pleased with the selfless act of Bheem, the forest dwellers majestically celebrated the marriage ceremony of their dear Hidimbi in hand with Bheem and graciously crowned him as the king of Kamyaka. After the celebrations were over, Bheem and Hidimbi embarked to the Pandavas settlement.

Hidimbi, adorned in white saree and varamaala, accompanied by Bheem, approached the griha where Pandavas are spending the exile. Draupadi dropped her jaw in astonishment seeing Hidimbi hand-in-hand with Bheem, and tumbled the vegetables she had cut for lunch and the copper plate onto the ground, unable to fill in the tint of shocked curiosity.

Bheem without a hint of trepidation reached Draupadi and introduced Hidimbi to Draupadi as her sister. Hidimbi, smiling tenderly in reverence with folded hands, greeted Draupadi. The noise, the tumbling copper plate had emanated, alerted others in the surroundings. The eldest, Yudhishthira was in deep philosophical debate with Sage Vyasa, Nakula was teaching various combinations of herbal remedies for deadly diseases to a group of forest children and Sahadeva was discussing the influence of the planetary motions on animal behavioural patterns with Krishna and Arjuna. Suddenly, all were drawn towards the echoing noise and hurriedly approached the hut only to get startled by seeing Bheem and Hidimbi together.

Everyone was shocked when Bheem introduced Hidimbi as his venerable wife and queen of Kamyaka forests. Nakula immediately felt the jolt when Bheem said, *queen of Kamyaka forests*. He recollected the incident that occurred during one of his interactions with his students. His students who were forest dwellers described the monstrous personality of the Kamyaka forest queen and the powers she acquired. They detailed that the queen was an exceptional sorcerer having the power to transform herself into any desired creature of any size. She can even become invisible, and produce a menacing army using distinct incantations. Nakula watched the gorgeous Hidimbi standing a few feet away, matching the description his students had given him.

Wary of the everyone's presence, without venting out any frustration that was seamlessly fuming on Draupadi's and Yudhishthira's faces, both welcomed Bheem and Hidimbi into their hut, instructing them to freshen up and finish post-marital rituals honouring the deities and departed souls.

Nakula noticed a null expression on the face of brother-in-law, Krishna and brother Sahadeva. He went towards them and inquired curiously, "Did you both by any chance know of Bheem's marriage well in advance?"

"What has prompted you to ask such a question?" quirked Sahadeva.

"The empty expressions marked as tall as a mountain on your faces." Nakula replied.

Krishna chuckled slyly and patted Nakula's shoulder, "It's the other way round, Nakula. In fact, I can't tell how happy I am for Bheem that he had chosen a lady for himself all by himself." Saying that, Krishna proceeded to a nearby tree where Draupadi, Yudhishthira and Arjuna were serving the people who accompanied Hidimbi and Bheem with the food they prepared for themselves.

Five-feet tall, oval-large eyes guarded by thick eye-brows, covered in chunky red sandalwood powder smeared all over the body. Neck confined by a large bead of hand-ball-sized skulls belonging to different kinds of animals. The Kamyakans seemed to bear no resemblance with Hidimbi as far as their physical descriptions are concerned, Nakula thought, watching Hidimbi's small entourage devouring the food. His thoughts, randomly recurring along the lines of the descriptions given by his tribal students and the appearances of the Hidimbi's followers. This perturbed Nakula. He gestured with dilated eyes for Draupadi to follow him. A bit apprehensive of the gesture, Draupadi shrugged at Nakula.

Nakula whispered, "This will only take a few moments of yours. Trust me. Please reach the distant tree where we used to soak our clothes."

Already irked, Draupadi curtly replied, "Fine." They moved towards the tree as Draupadi started to make a fuss and said, "Quickly, Nakula. I don't have much time. State the matter of your urgency that apparently can't seem to wait."

"Have you not been apprehensive that something sceptical...hm...implausible happened with brother Bheem?" He waited for the effect to show up in Draupadi's expressions, but she seemed uninterested. Nonetheless, Nakula continued, "I have a strong feeling, though Bheem might be huge and strong, he is still a child at heart."

"Come to the point, Nakula. I don't have all day to play with your riddles." said Draupadi.

"I think Bheem was tricked into marriage with her. I mean, honestly, something is not right with the dwellers." said Nakula.

"So, is everything right with the Pandavas?"

"No. Not that. I mean...,"

"Nakula, to clear your conscience, it's not innocence that your brother is permeated with, but infallible pride of strength. I have no doubt that she might have gotten the hint of it and smartly deceived him into her world with false admiration to which of course, as you all know, Bheem easily succumbed to that trap." Draupadi said in a vexed tone.

"But, can't we do anything about it? Are we meant to remain as mute spectators to this whole matrimonial deception?" questioned Nakula.

"Like my husbands remained mute spectators when I was disrobed openly?"

"Please. Draupadi. Not again, we are ashamed of the whole incident."

"Incident. Does it look like an incident to you?"

"I was not implying that"

"It was my honour, soul and self-respect that my husbands bargained away with. Not an incident. It was harsher than slaughter." Draupadi spewed angrily and continued, "Do you know the biggest sin this very heavenly earth carries, Nakula? That is to be born and voice one's opinion as a woman. No one had the audacity that includes my father, to question the very morale of having more than one husband to a single woman. It has occurred to me as if whole ingenious chauvinists, including the highly revered godlike celibate *Narada* were grouped to mould the logic by invoking the Sastras and Puranas into proving the sanctity of a single woman with five husbands was completely normal. At that juncture of time, even you did not dare to disagree with your mother, Kunti. Did you? No. At worst, no sane person had the decency to at least learn about my preference, my life, and my opinion. Not that I am unhappy being a wife to glorious Pandavas as the world admires you people, but

59

I am truly sorry to say that I was never treated as a human being. The human being capable of emotions, but treated as a prized possession always to play and jingle. Your brother, the precursor of Sastras, the forerunner of truth, the man of impeccable character, Yudhishthira, gambled away his wife, Nakula. Wife! Look me in the eye, Nakula. I am that wife, he gambled. Can you imagine?" taking a deep breath, Draupadi continued, "Can you imagine a lustful man winning your mother as a reward in gambling?"

Nakula lowered his head, and Draupadi continued, "But your brother gambled his wife away, as if I am his material possession to another narcissist, *Duryodhana*, in exchange for hoping to win the lost wealth and kingdom. A hope. Nakula...a hope. Because a thought crossed his mind to hope, and he wagered his wife in the gamble. Tell me Nakula, in those intoxicated moments of imprudent gambling, did you not feel that I was treated as a commodity of exchange available for a price?" Discerning the mummed expressions flaying on Nakula, Draupadi went on, "My distressed mind and aggrieved body were acutely deserted, when I realized that I was being dragged, that I was being stripped naked amongst the 'so called' pious seers, emperors, powerful influential individuals, courageous warriors and learned men. I repeat, not a single soul had the courage and character to defend the lone weak lumping woman begging for help while being dragged. I was squeezed and hung under my hair, strongly held and dragged by *Dushasana*. This barbaric cowardice act was openly performed and was joyfully spectated by the on looking brave men. However, the bards, the world, the society, the historical scriptures sing praises and narrate heroic stories about such kind of spineless men. Shame on the land that we are so proud of harnessing. It was my brother Krishna who rescued me in my helpless state and retained my womanhood, defying all the odds. It does not matter what the world brands Krishna as— a con man or a self-centred maniac, a womanizer or an illusionist, a trickster or a foreteller, or a God figure. But, to me, Krishna is the only living person who gives notable importance to every individual empathetically regardless of creed and sex. Coming to your brother, Bheem, I am glad that he has demonstrated maturity in safeguarding Hidimbi's emotions and interests which are clearly evident on Bheem's face. I cannot ascertain the motive in Hidimbi's mind that you are so much worried about, but I can certainly tell from her face that she has immense respect and love for Bheem. If a malignant situation arises, I can tell that she would move mountains and fight the Gods, if needed to protect Bheem. That much I can guarantee you with the intentions of Hidimbi that you are so much worried about, Nakula."

CHAPTER 9

The succour during the dreaded night of day one battle—

Owing to our added advantage at the end of day one of battle. We owe our lives to Yavaniens and our forefather's economic foresightedness that eventually lead us to possess the Castor-Bean plants.

Suprasena and I took a long stroll in our camp, supervising the burial of the soldiers we lost. The sight of blood dripping all over the ground, insides of the body ruptured left hanging out, blood-filled heads rolling on the grounds, soldiers with their half-cut bodies wailing and begging for a quick death incapable of bearing the raving pain, and some shocked and unconscious men were aimlessly walking with their severed-hands. The sight sent chills down our spines and made our bodies lethargic.

Departed soul's burial ceremony generally takes place in our city with their closed kins and kith's paying last rites and respects. The bull-cartels carrying the bodies are paraded all over the city for mourning. However, the present war offers no such lenience. If by any chance the cannibals manage to win the war, they would rampage without a second thought and feed on our dead bodies.

Keeping that presumption alive and fresh in our minds, during battle strategy Prahar, barring two dignitaries, everyone unanimously decided to cremate the body on the same day itself. This decision was taken to avoid being feasted upon losing the war. Mandakins (dead body cremators) and Priests were employed specifically to identify, collect, cremate and burn the bodies with proper Vedic prevalent rituals.

Half a Prahar past sunset, the bodies were towed to the central ground, arranged in a parallel order and cremated with ritualistic prayers, amidst the beatings of the drums, and furious soldier's long noises seeking vengeance for the lost lives.

After the large arrayal of cremation and bidding a soulful goodbye to the drifted souls, many soldiers went to have some good food and wine, some listened to bard's music and danced their troubles away, some took to meditation and prayers, while others succumbed to a deep slumber after a long overhauling tiring day.

Where food, wine and music are peculiar indulgences that will eventually lift the spirit of the soldiers for the next day's battle. In our kingdom, the induction of the *Dayadasini* during the battle-time has remained a contentious issue, since the inception of rules and ordeals concerning the life of the latter.

Dayadasini is a title given to those women who offer sensuous pleasures in return for silver coins and certain commodities. In the beginning, the commissioning of a Dayadasini was legalized as there was an obligated need felt for certain sections of women who were self-willing to pursue the duties and responsibilities that are required for a Dayadasini. The title of Dayadasini was regarded as challenging and daunting and considered as a reputed acquisition. After the title was conferred upon her, the woman would lose the identity that she acquired and was accustomed to since birth. Disinheriting the name she carried, dispossessing the relations she held, she would be called a Dayadasini.

Girls, post-puberty with the obtained procedural permissions from their parents were administered stringent training at the beginning of their careers. The training included practice and perfection of divergent forms of *Nritya* (dance forms), and music with wisdom over Ragas. Daily lessons were given to gain command over plant and animal anatomy, spiritual exercises principally involving the activation and understanding of *Muladhara chakra, Anahata chakra,* and *Sahasra chakra*. They even learnt behavioural psychology of human beings. These were taught by scholars who were responsible for teaching, guiding, testing, and finally bestowing the title of Dayadasini to the deserving women.

Many men, who were in powerful positions and could afford the services of a Dayadasini, characterized the women as stunningly beautiful, psychologically controlling, intelligent, and enchanting. The men became enslaved, to the pleasurable women's charm and their captivating caressing words. *As every household has a saying, "Every edible food raises higher and higher, right until the boiling point. From there on, it has to fall and fall and settle."* So was the case with the plight of a flourishing Dayadasini. Men of all sorts reached to the roost of a Dayadasini. However, these acts of the men infuriated the household women, who were gradually beginning to feel the withering of love away from them. This was evident from the men's demeanour. Soon, complaints started to reach the administration. The increasing priests occupying vital positions in the ruling administration played a major role by managing to create a perception of affixing sinister status to a Dayadasini, citing their actions to be a violation against Vedas and God's scriptures. They even prevailed in segregating the Dayadasini as an untouchable and a harbinger of sin.

With that shifted acumen, many women revolted against the Dayadasini's. They eventually dragged the women to the open streets, hurled abuses at them and beat them to a pulp. They even set fire to the learning centre and burned down the entire spectrum of Dayadasini culture to smear ashes. Post that incident, many Dayadasini's took shelter in temples of different villages and were left with no choice but to sustain life by begging, undertaking daily physical labour, and migrating to distant lands. After two decades of banning Dayadasini's, there was a general increase in women violations, rapes, and sexual harassment that was completely non-existent and minimal in the prevalent society.

My grandfather, Chitrasena, received numerous complaints from various women and formed an independent high-level committee. The committee consisted of twelve members— four locally elected citizen representatives of four separate divisions of the kingdom, two principal affluent women, one scholarly person, one woman from the Shudra community, two Brahmins holding important positions, and two principal students of the local Ashram. Suprasena was one of the constituted committees, being a student of *Roudrashudhi ashram.*

King Chitrasena instructed the committee to physically enquire about the ground-level practical facts. They were to interview the men and women of different strata regardless of caste or position, and submit the logical outcome of the committee report in thirty-four days.

The committee on final voting of seven agreements to five-disagreements submitted the detailed final report highlighting the principal reasons for rise in crime against women. It consisted of both biological and psychological factors. The report stated, "The growing sexual desire in men cemented with improper education during their natural upbringing with a near absence of value system, growing sense of inferiority complex, utter disregard and disrespect for women's societal importance and a perpetual chauvinistic attitude has been identified as the main reasons for the increase in physical abuse of women." The committee even made various observations by drawing comparisons between the time when Dayadasini's were rampant and the time of their complete isolation.

The report further stated that, "Dayadasini's were intelligent, psychologically potent, and perceptive about male's behaviour and their reaction. For the same reason, they were able to entertain with music and dance and exert immense psychological control over men's attitude with their sweet gestures and voice modulations as well as with their knowledge. These aspects drove the men to play to the tunes of a Dayadasini, resulting in the peaceful sensuous treatment of a male's growing sexual desires. However after the extinction of Dayadasini's, the desires of sexual nature and self-centred dominance fuelled in men's biological body. Without the required assistance of proper upbringing and conventional education with practical exposure to various societal norms, it made the ill-bantered men worse in harnessing their behaviour and attitude, gradually succumbing them to crime and abuse of women."

After carefully examining the entire committee report, Chitrasena, upon consultation with his principal advisors, *Ramakhetu* and *Vishnudar*, passed an abounding decree, declaring legal status to women employed as a Dayadasini. The act can neither be amended nor be scrapped for seven centuries. There was to be a complete reinstatement of the learning centre, allotment of a large scale of compensation to Dayadasini's and their affected families for the irrevocable damage caused by the errand citizens. Anyone who broke the decree will be awarded rigorous punishment consisting of drainage cleaning duties for fourteen long years. The persons directly or indirectly involved in prejudicial treatment to a Dayadasini or involved in provoking people to instil fear and hatred for the sole purpose of tarnishing the image of a Dayadasini will be treated accordingly as part of the punishment.

It took a year for the law to come into effect. The monthly crime report soon showed a gradual decrease in violence against women. Dayadasini's were given a respectable social and legal status in the society. Those Dayadasini's who had immense knowledge in warfare were approached by the king's planning ministry for timely advice and views and were paid handsomely for their services.

Since the inception of the law, and during the possibility of occurrence of war, a few Dayadasini's were employed to deviate the tired and psychologically weak men from war to exotic pleasures. After witnessing gruesome killing and dead bodies of their dear friends and soldiers, many of the tired and mentally hit men had taken refuge in the company of charismatic Dayadasini's to pass the night immersed in music and sensual pleasures.

After the burial rituals were finished, the two groups of four men each, who were tasked to find out the precise location of food essentials of Manikuntekans, were ordered to report to camp immediately. The directions that they have ventured into had proven fruitful. One group advanced in the northeast, tracked down the exact location of food storage and reported the same by locating the position in the map. *Manikuntekans growing weak and powerless. Hunger and inadequate food overwhelming their starving bodies. But, the results would show up probably on the third day of starvation, not*

forthwith. Yet, the ruin of their food essentials would definitely shatter their robust minds and bodies, I pondered.

Suprasena, gazing at the map with a mummed expression, started saying, "I mean, Manikuntekans are greedy cannibals. Alright. So, what would stop them from consuming the dead bodies of their fellow Manikuntekans. And let's assume the food essentials are somehow destroyed. They would become hysterical for sure. But, not for long as they will start feeding off their own dead army."

I accepted his line of thought and logical disposition. On the contrary, I felt not much of an effort will be drained. All it would take is a few sharp shooters and two rounds of attacks at the trenches of their food storage— one round for pouring wine and another for firing lighted arrows. So, I suggested going ahead with the chalked-out plan of destroying their food essentials.

Suprasena nodded in agreement and suggested the plan was to be executed one Prahar before sunrise. The action will frenziedly cause panic in the Manikuntekans leading them to chaos and confusion over the unavailability of food for the night and leaving them less time to strategize. This will eventually deliver us with an added advantage for the following day's battle.

CHAPTER 10

The tadpole of Kamyaka, 3149 BC

Sahadeva always gets a tinge of excitement whenever he gets to hear of Krishna's arrival. It is with him that he can freely engage in constructive arguments about life, soul, and life after death, astrology and music. Draupadi once in jest said to Krishna, "Sahadeva finds only you as the best company, only you as a contender, and as equal in knowledge to him. Better grace us with the secret, brother! We will follow the same path to become as good as you to Sahadeva."

Krishna grinned and replied, "Ha! He is modest. And I find my knowledge very inferior to nature. Nature strives consistently to provide sustenance and life and is at peace with the moment. In contrast, knowledge or the storage of information binds oneself to the past or into the near future. But, the moment will be missed. Mother Nature is materialized into many forms, a woman, a mother, a humble farmer, a cowherd, and..." Krishna was halted midway by Draupadi.

"Brother, I asked you a simple question. Yet, you are taking me on a world tour. It's either you are confused, brother, or I am beginning to slide into confusion with your twisting words of wisdom. Now please move to that garden where Sahadeva and Arjuna are waiting for you." With that, Draupadi made her way to water the garden of *crown* flowers that she was so lovingly nursing.

"Should I stay between you two intellects or be on my way?" Arjuna amiably said when Krishna approached him with a warm hug.

"You must stay and participate in the dialogues that we are about to have with each." replied Krishna. After exchanging pleasantries with each other, Krishna started playing *Alaap* with his wooden bansuri emanating *swaras* pulsating the surroundings with the rhythmic *raag*. Sahadeva, quickly comprehended the raaga that Krishna was playing, joined in with his wooden bansuri synchronizing the notes and the beat of that of Krishna's flute. Soon, the dim and sluggish wind started to soothe the floating birds in the clear sky. The horde of yellow-faced parrots and a few white-feathered peacocks closed in, oscillating with the emanating music.

Catching the sound and sensing the arrival of his uncle with the emanating music from the Bamboo flute, five-year-old *Ghatotkacha* with his small steps, bolted towards Krishna tracing the sound. Reaching near him, he stood silently and marvelled at the *raag* that was being played. Immediately after the parrots scampered into the sky, and the peacocks vacated to their nesting places, after the climax of the raaga, Ghatotkacha grilled Krishna with lots of questions, "Uncle, what raaga are you playing? Can you teach me? What mood and emotion, the raag emulates?" gasping for air in the tinge of excitement, Ghatotkacha continued, "And what have you brought for me, uncle? Why have you not come for three years? Did my brother Abhimanyu send any messages? Did you tell him that I am dying to meet him?"

CHAPTER 11

The dwellings of the past—

After the long overhauling tiresome day, I immersed myself in a hot wooden tub bath, the most desired need in a turbulent time. My body and every bit of my achy muscles felt relaxed, with a few bruises making stinging sensations with the touch of hot water, albeit pleasant they were. I gently closed my eyes and rested my head over the edge of the tub, with my bare legs spread out, gently resting under the warm water. *The sight of many dead and the wailings of the families and the children, many perturbed thoughts begin to flash, disorienting my mind's equilibrium until the sight of my dear Rasikri pleasingly stunned my afflicted soul.*

I can still remember the last time that we had a bath together. It was like it happened yesterday. The smell of her alluring skin embraced in my caressing hold, cuddling each other, our hands clasped together with sensuous expelling laughs. Her long bronze-coloured knee-length hair breezed through my right ear, criss-crossing through my chin with our unadorned bodies intact. Those quiet moments felt surreal, with bewildered jubilation victimizing and preying upon us. We felt surrounded with love, in those silent spectacles of making love.

I watched Rasikri grow right from childhood into a mature, elegant, intelligent and uniquely stellar woman. She was well versed in staff-fighting using a double stick. Her parents did not have a steady influx of income being agricultural labourers, constantly worried about their only daughter's upbringing. One more complication had been added into their already discorded life when they realized the boundless potential and intellect Rasikri possessed. They understood, these qualities of hers are quite uncommon for a fourteen-year-old girl who was born into the family of the impoverished. Their apprehension grew steadily when they observed the morbid envy that came across from the immediate families in their locality. They were sure that if Rasikri came into the limelight using her intellect, she would be bound to infuriate peers and seniors belonging to higher castes and other sects of the society.

Hugh! Intelligence. Intelligence. Society can afford to tolerate poverty, illiteracy, and famines but cannot risk the very existence of intelligence anywhere in its proximity, I pondered.

Rasikri's spiralling unique rationale day by day started to deliver accolades to her. But, the accolades compelled her parents to safeguard her more. They presumed her talents might intimidate the convictions of the society, eventually branding her as intolerant to society. No doubt, her parents were always in awe of the prodigious Rasikri. Whenever they had a chance to witness Rasikri engage herself in an intellectual debate with assiduous pupils of her age, happiness has no limits for them. However, this did not stop them from worrying with the constant fearful thought circling in their minds.

Whenever acquaintances and strangers acknowledged and lauded the efficacy of Rasikri, they felt immensely proud. Although, at the same time they were worried as they were well aware of the certain vulnerabilities of having a prodigy in society that can infuriate people belonging to higher social status, who expect only their descendants to have dominion over intellectual wisdom and never a low born to achieve the highest learning and proficiency. For they know, knowledge harnessed with the right attitude alone can secure a high position of power in society. Her parents couldn't help but allow Rasikri to take active part in local debates organized by highly acclaimed priests of the kingdom. She often excelled and brought home the prized possessions consisting of an abundance of fruits, rice, wheat, and adornments. The rewards gradually eliminated their hunger, and their respect among the society has manifold increased.

Among the one-hundred and fourteen competitions organized so far, Rasikri, with her philosophical wisdom and proficiency, had defeated eighty-three Vedic scholars of all ages. The bulk of the contestants either belonged to Brahmins or Kshatriyas. Rasikri becomes quite popular for being the only shudra and the only girl among the nine women participants out of two hundred. One among the contestants who always emerged to the last available round was *Gyanvitarna*, seven years elder to Rasikri.

Gyanvitarna was the son of the renowned academician *Goklevitarna*, one of four principal advisors to king Chitrasena. Gyanvitarna, since his childhood, on the contrary had a deep passionate adulation towards art and sculpture. However, upon the forceful insistence and will of his father he had to turn his mind to Vedas that he utterly hated to learn.

Whenever he had the threshold of time after finishing the classes of mugging-up Vedas, he along with a few of his friends who had similar interests, travelled to the nearby hills and started carving beautiful sculptures. His art depicted animals on the run, women feeding, children playing and many more. As time turns the tide, the sculptures stood no chance of secrecy and were soon discovered by some pedestrians. They immediately rushed to the kingdom and conveyed this information to one chief-caretaker of my mother Chitrangada, the only daughter of Samrat Chitrasena. Having learned about the fascinating sculptures from the chief-caretaker, my mother instructed the latter to accord guest status to the pedestrians who had delivered the information. Guest status included offering lavish accommodation for a three-night stay, having delicious food of choice and a personal tourist guide to acquaint with the city.

My mother herself being a painting prodigy couldn't help but get intrigued and was equally excited to witness the narrated carved sculptures herself. She always had a niche and love for nature and never hushed away from capturing nature's dazzling radiance into her paintings. She had a large collection of self-drawn paintings numbering around thirteen hundred kept in a large private hall. Some paintings were as tall as eighteen feet. The enticing classiness could only be felt when witnessed from close quarters. One look at her paintings, her soul for a quick snap of time is silently revealed.

In one of her collections, a painting of *Goddess Parvathi* dressed in a *green saree* offering a mouthful of water to a group of lambs and predators had bewildered my dozing senses into inconceivable imaginations. I enquired with my mother about the gravity of depth involved with this particular painting. She explained about the mysterious ways and works that nature engages herself in. She tenderly said, "Son, Goddess Parvathi is the personification of the gracious mother nature in human form. For her, every living being is her loving child. Her nurture towards her children is and will be devoid of any distinction and discrimination." Gently walking towards the right corner of the painting, she continued, "The green saree she is dressed in characterizes the colours of mystified nature."

"Then what is God, Ma and why do people refer to him or her as the all-powerful and benevolent?" I probed with new germinating curiosity.

"Babru, God is a mundane idea created, established and conceived by the insidious people to please the whims of society and give the powerful a peculiar hold over the meek, weak, innocent and ignorant. So, the idea of God glues to every soul like a thread but controlled by a few." She held my hand, walked me out into the open, where she made me sit and placed her hand over my shoulders. She then looked at the sky and she continued, "Look at the sun, the sky, the butterflies and the birds, what do you see, son?"

Confused with her words, I ran a quick gaze at the sky and said, "Ma, what are you implying? I see the sun, sky, butterflies and birds as they are."

Grinning at my looming confusion and holding me tighter, she said, "Watch carefully, Babru. I see pure joy dancing in the air. I see elation. I see no qualms, worries, distress or pretence in their living."

More confused, I further asked, "How Ma?"

She gently smiled and replied, "They live in the moment, Babru. They just live the moment. That's where God lies. That's where Godliness prevails."

So joy it is, I thought and asked, "Then what is God, Ma?"

"O' you are so full of questions." she tenderly smiled, pinched my cheeks and continued, "A true God is of neither form nor name but a pure action born out of naught silence. A true God is but a luminous energy found anywhere and everywhere in the form of emotions, love, caring, art, music, helping the needy, feeding the hungry, nurturing nature, sheltering the weak."

I was transfixed. I was just transfixed as I used to be every time, listening to her words, in her translucent voice, with her calm and serene eyes, as if her silence was conveying me more and more messages.

Mother quickly dressed herself with a light-blue cotton saree with its loose end draped over her left shoulder and a shining white-gold thin chain dangling around her neck with a small diamond embedded in it. The white gold was quite rare in the region as nature did not deem it fit for humans to possess it. However, during one of my grandfather's voyages to the kingdom of *Vidarbha* in central Bharatkanda. He was graced by the king of Vidarbha with the formula to yield white gold. He passed this formula to our exquisite goldsmiths. The latter blended silver to yellow-gold in the required ratio to yield the white-gold. The process involved dedicated effort and spending of coins, but grandfather opined that mother was righteously worthy of possessing the precious white gold.

Mother greeted the guest-informants with a firm smile, acknowledging them with a Namaste. She promised them the gifts in the form of silver coins and lots of cereals once having assessed the sculptures herself. The informants were offered the horse cart and mother, as usual rode her white horse, which she had named *Abhakshi*, meaning the first ray of light. *I will be forever oblivious to her never-ending obsession with the colour white. Only God can understand her mystery filled mind.* The informants led my mother and accompanied soldiers into the thick forest and halted near the huge deep parallel arranged rocks, paving the way to the linear falling water heaving from the hilltop. The place was pulsating with echoes of babbling birds and water droplets. Walking further into the forest, she saw the blurred rock depictions through the tree as she quickened her steps, moving closer and closer. As soon as she reached, my mother was spellbound with her jaw dropped in disbelief, witnessing the extravagantly made enticing sculptures. The sheer imitation and reflection of human emotions carved on the dead rocks provoked tears of euphoria. She was under a magical spell, marvelling at the intensity of emotions emulated in the carved sculptures, depicting– a mother cultivating the agricultural land and breastfeeding her new-born baby with her elated smile intact. Restless wealthy king unable to rest adequately with all the available luxuries while a homeless beggar was in deep slumber amidst dust with torn clothes. And Goddess Saraswathi sitting exuberantly adjacent to a person playing the musical instrument Veena.

All the ingenuity was resonated in the sculptures toying with the notions of provoking one's senses into the vast design of spiritualism. After breaking out from the chiselled spell, mother immediately rushed to the kingdom and ordered the spies to dig and enquire about the craftsperson responsible for the sculptures. After taking orders, the nine spies rushed to the spot of sculptures and kept three persons in constant lookout, disguising themselves ninety-feet away. Meanwhile, the rest of the spies rushed to every available ashram, enquiring about any person trained in the art of sculpture. Every reply to their query was meted out with either "They don't teach sculpture" or with a vague "No."

Upon learning about some specific persons belonging to the king's chambers and enquiring about the rock sculptures, Gyanvitarna and two of his friends hurried to the forest to scrutinize the condition of the sculptures with the constant lurking fear spiralling in their hearts. They suspected that the sculptures were vandalized. They breathed a sigh of relief after they realized that the sculptures were safe. The one thing they did not pay attention to was that they were constantly being watched and their physical identity was compromised to the disguised spies lying low in the forest. After Gyanvitarna and his friends cleared the area, the spies kept pace with the Gyanvitarna horses keeping a distance and followed them right into the falling moon to their respective homes splitting themselves in between. With the sun hitting the first ray, the spies proceeded to the queen's quarters and gave a detailed report about the identities of the three persons they pursued all night long and were positive of their involvement in the sculptures.

Mother appreciated the spies for their quick, witty, and smart approach to the assigned task and promised them a lifetime of care for their children. While she was going with the given names, she was shocked to learn that the son of Goklevitarna popped up in one of the names amongst the three. She hurried to the king's chambers and enquired about the whereabouts of Goklevitarna. She proceeded in the pointed direction and found Goklevitarna, other personnel advisors, and the king Chitrasena deeply engrossed in a conversation. Realizing mother's presence, they suddenly stopped their grooving conversation, paving way to the awe of silence. Grandfather and the others welcomed my mother and gently enquired about the reason for her sudden showing-up. Mother with a tiny grin replied to my grandfather, "Oh! It was nothing father, I had a small curious inquiry. " Saying that she gently turned to Goklevitarna and curiously asked about why he never got the chance to mention about his son being a skilful sculptor.

Everyone in the private chamber jolted back and widened their eyes. A dismayed expression was etched on everyone's face. They told her that they even did not have the slightest knowledge of this. Especially since they were all colleagues and old friends. There must have been some misunderstanding, they said.

Goklevitarna, clearing all the air and confusion, assured my mother that he himself did not know and reiterated that had he known, he would have shared this information with the king himself. He was confident that his son had never spoken about sculptures at home and all his indulgences were in Vedic scriptures.

Mother stood up and requested Goklevitarna just to have a word with his son and if possible, to introduce him along with his two friends to her the next morning. Goklevitarna folding his hands in Namaste, replied, "Sure, queen."

CHAPTER 12

The incessant light—

Krishna analysed Ghatotkacha for a while— his strong legs, increased height to five feet, long curly hair, broad shoulders, and large eyeballs with thickened eyebrows, obtuse nose, and giant ears. Krishna said, "Cool down. Ghatu. Cool down. I am not going anywhere." Cuddling Ghatotkacha in the round belly and moving from left side to right side, Krishna continued, "Look at you growing at the speed of light to be a mighty muscular being. Coming to your unending queries, let me try to answer them one by one. Your brother Abhimanyu passed his love and well-wishes to you. In fact, he asked me to draw a painting of you using coal and bring it to him. Secondly, the raag that I am rendering is *Raag Bhairavi.* The raag evokes the emotions of love and passion for the omniscient God, or it could be for any person that one loves or for the teacher he admires. You can bring the *Veena* that your mother specifically made for you so that I can teach you right away. Now Ghatu, tell me about all the things that you have been learning these three years."

"Uncle, I am exuberant to play raag Bhairavi. My mother has kept me busy all these years. She taught me daily household activities such as cleaning dishes, serving food, and washing my own clothes. She emphasizes meditating on goddess mother Kali at least

83

once a day for a prahar and whenever my father finds time, he vigorously trains me for Malyudh (combat wrestling) and teaches me how to wield the weapon, *Gadha*. Badi-ma (Draupadi) has taught me Alankaras for one straight year and then principal ragas with the instrument *Veena*." cackled Ghatotkacha with a big cleft forming on the right cheek.

Arjuna said, "Ghatu, tell uncle Krishna about your education and meditating experience on mother Kali." With a small pat on his shoulders.

"I will be pleased, father." Heeding to Arjuna's advice, Ghatotkacha asked Krishna, "You might remember the last time you were here, Uncle. You, mother, Badi-ma, everyone and Gurudev Vyasa Maharshi were discussing life and God."

Krishna, with a hint of doubt, replied, "Since it was a long time ago. Hm. I guess a little of what I remember."

"In that discussion, you were explaining the prerogative of the entire universe and the ruminative conscious individual becoming one and the same. The awakened Rishi who meditates and focuses all his energy on *Ajna chakra*, a point on the forehead between the eyebrows. You said to them, 'the duality of life is veritably non-existent.'" Ghatotkacha continued with a tinge of excitement, "Your plain talk about the dual-natured world and the oneness has expounded some deeper truths and had a dwelling impact upon my consciousness."

In awe of what he was witnessing, bewildered, Krishna gazed into Arjuna and Nakula's eyes in quick succession and gasped, "Are these words of a five-year-old boy? Or a living ascetic?"

"Not the time to let your heart and mind wander to astonishment. You are yet to be stumped, *Murali Manohara* (other name of Krishna)..." Nakula grinned at Krishna and asked Ghatotkacha to continue.

"So, uncle. After you departed, I requested my mother to explain in detail about chakras, the theory of duality and single-mindedness. Mother elucidated about *Sahasra Chakra* and *Muladhara Chakra.*" Ghatotkacha replied.

"So, what have you learned, Ghatu?" asked Krishna

"That to arrest *Sahasra chakra*, one needs to primarily awaken the *Muladhara chakra*, which is the root essence of all creation and signifies the emotion of smell. It is pertinent to control the energy churned out from this chakra using various *mudras* and body postures in order to bring focus to higher chakras. Hence, I gained theoretical knowledge about the essence of breath in one's life. The body that we dwell in, the body that we so carefully nurture was simply a lifeless structure without breath. So, I mastered the frequency of inhalation and exhalation with an erect spine, seated in *Siddhasana* with *Yoni* mudra and after a few days of a daily dose of meditation, I was finding it difficult to concentrate and hold my thoughts in control. That's when *Badi-ma* advised me to concentrate on cardinal energy close to my heart. The reference of concentration might be a human form or any form or completely formless state. She precisely told me not to channel my energy on controlling thoughts rather was told to witness them as a separate entity as observing the dawning thoughts as you observe the ripples on a river. Heeding to Badi-ma's advice, I have chosen mother Kali to centre all my energy by chanting - *Om Kring Kalikaye namah* that my mother chants all the time."

"Then...." Krishna ushered in a curious tone.

"After a few months of my meditation, mother Kali appeared and blessed me with her radiating aura and presence. The sight of her illuminated pitch dark physical appearance covered in a plain red saree with the yellow border running horizontally, her large caressing eyes, paving the way to a sharp nose that is hitched with a broad golden nose ring; this magnanimous sight of her, shuddered my nerves. With her distinctive motherly voice, she called me with her open arms. I bowed in reverence and drowned myself into her arms, seated on her right lap. In that buoyant love, she has become my mother." said Ghatotkacha.

Shocked to incredulity, jaw dropped to amazement, with eyeballs exploding to implausible feet, Krishna was thunderstruck and at loss of words. This kind of conscientious collapse occurs very rarely in Krishna's life. Marking the silence that surrounded Krishna's senses, Nakula shook Krishna's shoulders to normalcy and informed Ghatotkacha to leave and help mother Hidimbi and Badi-ma Draupadi with their works.

After Ghatotkacha's departure to his mother's, Krishna murmured in bewilderment, "Arjuna, what I just witnessed and heard from the little child is not a normal phenomenon. Either Lord Shiva himself has taken birth in Ghatotkacha's form or he is the Tandava (Celestial dance) himself. Such immaculate pureness, a body with a devoted spirit, a mind without a speck of dust. On one side, we have Abhimanyu, who is a distinct prodigy in every field he sets his focus on and on the other we have Ghatotkacha, his curly smile with pristine heart, his untainted prayer even could not stop Goddess Kali from embracing him. This world is not yet ready for such exceptional lights. We must at any cost protect them at all costs."

Draupadi cut in on the conversation from behind Krishna by nudging him on his back and joined the gathering by saying, "Brother, hope my son Abhi and sister Subhadra are doing great. My son Ghatu portrayed the whole development that transpired here and I could not hold my curiosity anymore, so I rushed here to witness your astounded expression."

"Yeah...yeah...even I am surprised to see you growing backwards."

"I didn't get you, brother."

"See your husbands with their deepening wrinkles and you on the other hand are growing beautiful with each passing day."

"O' *Kanha*. Stop your teasing. I very much understand your unique craft of diverting a talking point." Draupadi mocked Krishna teasingly.

"You two, please. Not again. Half your life was already history yet the child in you both cannot stop bantering with each other." Nakula revelled at them both and continued, "Kanha, let me clear your apprehension about Ghatu. Bheem and Hidimbi have already decided and arrived at a consensus that it's in the best interests of Ghatotkacha that Hidimbi and Ghatu continue to stay in the Kamyaka forests even after the fourteen-year exile of the Pandavas gets completed. Brother Bheem for a long time did not approve of the idea but finally acceded, witnessing the agility with which Ghatotkacha is flourishing. So technically, after the exile, Ghatotkacha will be crowned the youngest king of the Kamyaka forests."

"Hm....that's in the best interests of everybody. Otherwise, only the Lord knows what this wickedest world will conspire of Ghatotkacha, if the society gets a whiff of his powers." said Krishna and with the air of relief, he gently moved towards Arjuna and continued, "Arjuna, I also feel, you make the best utilization of this exile as Sage Vyas had rightly advised. I recommend you reach deep into the foot of the Himalayan Mountains by moving through the northeast of Kamyaka forests. Once you realize, you have crossed paths with sages and austere tapaswis (ascetics), then it's certain that you have reached the mountains of *Indrakila*. Make the divine place as your abode of performing austerity. The mountain brims with the vibes of divinity and vivid natured illusions. Don't be lured into a spider web of enticing illusions. They were abnormal eruptions occurring irregularly as a result of extreme austerity by the Tapaswis. Everything that happens in the mountains will not make sense to your logical mind. You will start listening to trees speaking and the animals conversing. Pay no heed to the happenings around you. You are bound to get deviated, if your mind starts thinking about the illusionary circumstances around you. Just focus all your energy on Lord himself and the acquisition of divine weapons."

CHAPTER 13

The rarity and a prodigy—

After bidding a goodbye to his friends, Gyanvitarna returned home taking a sigh of relief upon knowing the safety of the sculptures. He was confused to find his father staring suspiciously at him and his mother nervously puncturing her nails. Gyanvitarna discerned something had turned the tables upon him and was trying hard to recollect the various probabilities of mischiefs done by him that might have reached the ears of his father and subsequently infuriated him. Gyanvitarna slowly moved forward, taking tiny steps with innocent eyes gulped inside. He enquired reverently, "Father, what might have happened that has caused so much silence at home? Do I have any part in it?"

Goklevitarna slowly turned to look right into Gyanvitarna's eyes, staring for a long while and then in a controlled tone said, "Gyanvi, I would like to ask you a few questions that are obviously causing me trouble since the mid-sun prahar and I expect the truth and only the truth to be told without a quiver or a mild body tremor. Am I understood, Gyanvi?"

"Yes, father." Gyanvitarna said quietly. In those few moments, his mind was stunned into silence yet, he couldn't help but feel a lot of questions popping up in his mind in those moments of silence. *What possibly could I have done that infuriated father to no bounds? The bodily behaviour that is on open display is very uncommon or for that matter, this is the very first time. What role do I have in that 'God knows what incident' that irked father so much that it forced my mother into silence, drawing her continuous blabber and chatter into queer silence.*

After a few moments of naught silence, "Gyanvi, are you in any way trying to conceal something related to your passion or a long-carried hobby from me? If yes, this will be the last chance you will get to divulge the information to me. Else, tomorrow or some other day for that matter, if that passion or hobby reaches my knowledge from a source other than you, that includes your mother, I will cast you to far south *Malyavat* forests for eighteen long years. Few soldiers will accompany you for forty-eight days to drop you in the midst of the forest. Therefore, let this message be ingrained inside your mind before you answer. So, I will give you a few moments to ponder over the deep seriousness of it and answer." Saying that Goklevitarna leaned back in the chair.

Shivering at the thought of repercussions he was about to face, Gyanvitarna mumbled for words and fell very short of breath. In those tense moments of adversity, Gyanvitarna realized that his sculpting and the soldier's interrogation and his father's probing are not mere coincidences but an interconnected occurrence. He was pretty sure the sculpting had reached his father's ears. So, Gyanvitarna decided to lie about his art and stammered, "fa....ther, I und....erstand....that yo...u are refer....refe...rin...g to sculp....ting. I swear my life to

91

you, I hard.....ly make the best u.....u..se of available time to le.....learn Veda..s and scriptur...es."

"Son. Have some hot water and take a few deep breaths. It will ease your strain and you can present your thoughts lucidly." His mother said while offering him some water. Gyanvitarna was very much aware that mere explanation cannot satiate his stern father but a firm, logically constructed elucidation will do the consolation. So, after gulping a sip of water, Gyanvitarna continued, "Father, I hardly get any spare time after spending half my day learning the scriptures. Thereafter, I start preparing for the Vedic fairs conducted very frequently. Gaining a dominant position in those Vedic fairs is crucial and paramount as the Vedic fair is considered to be of paramount importance in our family prestige since the times of our forefathers. We have never lost the title but I have. I have failed our family. And now I carry the weight of dignity on my shoulders." saying that Gyanvitarna observed the changing expressions on his father's face into normalcy and continued with more boldness, "Father, as you are well aware, since the past year I have been losing to one girl. She belongs to the lowest societal lineage. Although I am adjusted to the second position, I cannot tell how much the defeat to a girl is stabbing my heart and tearing my soul into fragments." Gyanvitarna observed the furious fumes of embarrassment profiling on his father's face at the mention of defeat to a low caste girl, "Nevertheless, now I am prepared more than ever and I am routing all my energy into preparing for the contest that is due for forty-eight days from now."

In a prided toned pitch, "I never doubted your competence, son." and then Goklevitarna continued with a distasteful prejudice, "But, sculpting. Ugh! When Queen Chitrangada asked for my knowledge about you being a sculpture. My immediate feeling was full of loathing for my failure at your upbringing. Only the shunned and mortified individuals will pick such occupation, art or amusement whatever. That's precisely my reason for being so hard on you, son. But, the only question that pricks me is why would they doubt you or for that matter, even bring up your name, son?"

Rage seething from inside at the blatant ignorant remarks made by his father about the beauty of sculpting. Gyanvitarna thought *it would take eons for him to even understand one-hundredth of the sculpture art. He should be considering himself lucky for having come across the art in his proximity. How could he know? The man spent the better part of his life in the shadows of attachment to power. How would he know? For he never had the insight to assimilate the simple beauties of life joyously, nor had he the experience of the rarefied moments of sculpting in which one would find himself in union with the entire spectrum of the universe. I pity the self-driven man, for he cannot even have the glimpse of what I have embraced. I feel sorry for this poor soul, for he can never even remotely comprehend the joyous intimacy I am acquainted with every stroke that I indulge in during sculpting.*

After gaining composure, Gyanvitarna said, "Father, if my activity has brought disgrace to your position or respect. I would happily receive any punishment that you deem fit for me. But father, it was my close friend *Bhatukesh,* who has an obsession with sculpting."

Suddenly the image of the dark obtuse figure, with uneven curly hair spread over unevenly, cheeks as round as moon started to emerge in the subconscious mind of Goklevitarna and after a few moments of silence, with a shocking expression exclaimed, "Are you by any chance referring to that hopeless creature whose only aim in life seems to accumulate more and more food in his own belly?"

"Yes," nodded Gyanvitarna.

Laughing out loud and taken aback by the remarkable image of Bhatukesh, Goklevitarna commented, "Hmm! quite shocking that a blockhead can muster the strength and time to carve a stone. Alright, Son. I will inform the queen about the blockhead." Kissing Gyanvitarna's forehead, Goklevitarna started off towards the kingdom to pass on the news.

CHAPTER 14

Kairata Parva, 3149 BC

"I was ruminating about this for a long time now, Vasudeva (other name of Krishna). I must start to prepare for my departure then, maybe four days from today to the abode of the Indrakila Mountains." Arjuna beamed with the thoughts of meditation and Lord Shiva's virtue of presence.

"Nakula, you have been to Indrakila once. Please brief the route, essentials that are to be carried, the shifting of temperatures and the requisite rest and the time for Arjuna's journey." requested Krishna.

"Sure. Kanha." Nakula moved to Arjuna and said, "Brother. Follow the river *Saraswathi* from our forest until it breaks up into four daughters. Before reaching the auspicious *Ramatirtha* village, you will arrive at *Vadarapachana*, the village of the unique collection of flowers and fruits in abundance. The place is distinguished for two reasons. One, Lord Indra had married a Brahmacharin (celibate) there. Two, the longest drought of twelve years engulfed the village. You need to rest there for a day and upon receiving the blessings of Lord Indra in a nearby temple, take eastward direction and follow the course of Saraswathi right up to the fourth daughter. Be cautious of moving south from where the kingdom Kuru starts. Even the

95

slightest knowledge of your presence will alert the Kauravas and will restore our fourteen-year-long exile right from the beginning."

"Oh! I thought you were beginning to enjoy exile." giggled Arjuna.

Everyone laughed lightly and Nakula continued, "Leave behind my likes. I am very sure brother Bheem would be happier if our exile gets extended."

"Yeah. Yeah. You even started to produce offspring from the river Saraswathi. 'Tributaries' are way better than to be called daughters, I suppose." Bheem sarcastically remarked at Nakula.

Nakula said, 'Ha! I will try then, brother Bheem." He moved his focus to Arjuna and continued, "Just at the start of the fourth daughter. Sorry. The fourth tributary of river Saraswathi."

"I advise you to spend the rest of your life with hills and mountains. I am sure, the mountains are having few children of their own." With that comment of Bheem's, everyone burst into endless laughter.

After a moment's indulgence in fun and banter, Nakula said, "Can I?" He looked at everyone's faces until settling on Arjuna and continued, "Brother. River Saraswathi breaks into two tributaries, one flowing north and the other flowing south. You will realize at the collision of two opposite paralleled courses, the colour of the river slightly changes to light-blue due to the heavy colliding force of the opposite flowing waters. You will find translucent water with no fishes or any kind of dirt in that particular spot, allowing you to see clearly beneath the river. So, stop at that locus, cross the river and move in a southeast direction right until you find a place called *Shamachakra*, just before you hit the river *Drishadvathi*."

"Please be very mindful in Shamachakra. As you are well aware, Kauravas frequently visit to Shamachakra to periodically check on the adequate strength of the installed formidable gates and rock structures at the border, fearing the intrusion of Naga tribes. The land of the *Nagas* lies in the vast forests spread between the river *Yamuna* to the west, flanked by Kurukshetra and River *Ganga* to the east binding the Kingdom of *Panchala*." cautioned Draupadi to Arjuna

"From Shamachakra onwards, travel in the north-east direction, avoid the path leading to Drishadvathi River. You will start experiencing abnormal shifting temperatures, longer nights and a shorter duration of sunlight. Ensure to keep your body warmer, either by indulging in speed walking or dands or light body movements. Else the cold waves will freeze your organs, subsequently stopping your heart from beating. From here on, you cannot rely on a vegetarian diet. You must adopt an animal diet that will supply adequate proteins into your body and help preserve the body in a lukewarm state, enough to keep your muscles from shrinking— *a wide variety of fish, hunting down boars and musk deer's are preferable and common in this area*. After a few days of traveling, you will reach the river Ganga. Cross the river and reach the head of *Panchala* Kingdom. From there on, advance in the northern direction and you will start finding Lotus flowers,

Blackbucks and the rarest species of black-bodied Peacocks. You will then be involved with a sudden rise in temperatures, large trees and many ascetics meditating. Just know that you have finally reached the heavenly abode of Indrakila Mountains. The mountain is approximately eight thousand steps above sea level." With a tiny grin, Nakula continued, "And I request Vyas Maharshi to let brother Arjuna be acquainted with all the proper methods in performing the austerity." With that appraisal and instructions, Nakula resumed himself to be seated next to Krishna.

Vyas Maharshi was circling his rudraksha one bead after another, half-closed his eyes as he resonated, "Om Shivaya Namah." and moved his eyes in the direction of Arjuna and said, "*Dhananjaya* (other name of Arjuna), once you reach Indrakila mountains, collect as many fruits as possible to rejuvenate your body. This is needed during your steadfast meditation. You will discover manifold white marbles gracing the land. When the Sun is shutting its light onto the mountains, the last feeble rays will reflect on a large white marble. Go there, pay obeisance to Shiva linga and start walking towards where Lord Nandi points at. You will reach for a small opening leading to a large cave. The cave is the place of your confinement for performing the meditative austerity on Lord Shiva. This particular cave has a continuous supply of freshwater, owing to its source in the Himalayan Mountains. The water is revitalized continuously on its way from the large mountains, being exposed to the touch of countless naturally found chemicals. Hence, the fresh water thus found in the caves turns neon-blue every so often. Camouflage all your weapons inside of a large trunk of a tree in the cave. Thereupon, select a corner. Sit in a westerly direction, design a palm-sized Shiva linga with the mud. Place this red amulet surrounding the Shiva linga at the base and tip." Handing the amulet in the extended hands of Arjuna, Gurudev continued, "This particular amulet is energized with the *Gayathri mantra* for one hundred and eight days at *Somnath temple*. I am handing it over in your care now."

Arjuna, pondering over the journey and the practice of austerity on Lord Shiva. He enquired further, "Gurudeva, when should I be taking breaks to satiate my daily bodily needs? Shall I skip or reduce meals to prove my unflinching devotion to Lord Shiva? And how to keep track of time? What if my senses stop responding to hunger or thirst? What if I slowly fail my body and die, completely immersed in austerity? Please enlighten me with your wise words, Gurudeva."

With a mild grin, Maharshi Vyas replied, "O' *Arjuna Phalguna*, your troubled mind is no exception to this immense, arduous and exhausting austerity that you are committing into. Many exceptional seers before you struggled the same way as you before embarking on the journey of an ascetic. Remember, once you commence your single-minded meditation on *Lord Someshwara* (Other name of Shiva), you will begin to witness your whims, your desires will have no control over your senses. Once you are bestowed with the blessings of

Lord Someshwara's physical presence, you are bound to be captivated under the spell of Lord himself. You will dissolve in his ethereal trance, much the same as many myriad small, large, calm flowing and heavy-thrashing innumerable rivers confluence together, ultimately merging into the mammoth ocean. The Lord himself will release you from your spellbound trance and will confer you with the destructor of seven worlds, the *Pashupatastra* without you even asking for it. So Arjuna, your troubled mind is completely understandable. I reckon Krishna is the best person to resolve all your prying questions."

CHAPTER 15

The approach towards the second day of the war—

My myriad thoughts of reminiscing were interrupted by Suprasena visiting my chambers and calling me for supper. Drying my soaked hair with warm smoke, I greeted Suprasena with a pat on his shoulder and walked together to the commonly arranged open dining area. At times of war, we had emphasized no distinctions, no special treatments nor any kind of exclusive attention depending on the military stature or any royal power holders. Let it be the infantry or the caretakers, the commanders or the Dayadasini's, the kings or the court physicians. Everyone is to be treated equally while a piece of the meal is being served. The only diet rule we have set for everyone during times of war is to have ample food needed for rejuvenation of the tired body. The diet consisted primarily of three bananas, a mix of staple food, coconut water and goat meat. Excess eating was not encouraged principally for the sole reason of becoming slow and slumber during the battle. Any kind of greetings was forbidden during dining to enable the soldiers focus on the diet that is crucial for the exasperated muscles that will prove to be very gainful during the war for the following day.

After we finished the food chores, I called out for a brief meeting between me, the commanders and Suprasena about chalking out the strategy for the next day. Suprasena was standing to my right, chief-military-commander Durvasana was seated opposite me and respective commander-in-chief's of Patyadhakshas (Infantry), Ashvadhyakshas (Archers), Rathadhyakshas (Cavalry) and *Astabhargava*—our kingdoms principal military expert and strategist for past forty-eight years. All exchanged greetings and made themselves comfortable at the circular table. I mildly nodded at Suprasena to start the proceedings. With a reflective nod, Suprasena fetched the large rectangular map, spread it over the table and began the opening deliberation by paying last respects to the martyrs, appreciating the brave effort put up by the soldiers. It gave them the added advantage in lifting the spirits of the soldiers and in neutralizing the numbers at both sides. With that comment, everyone in the room prided themselves with raised chests and thumping on the table, signalling their gratification for the recently departed soldiers and contentment on day one battle.

I interjected Suprasena for a moment and announced to all the members present, three generations of special care were to be provided to the surviving families of the martyrs in the form of medical, education, skill development and upbringing. Everyone around the table nodded in agreement and the chief of Patyadhakshas said, "That is the least we can do to the immediate family, for the sacrifice rendered for the safety of our kingdom. I hope the brave spirits are happily watching over us." and I positively acknowledged his kind words and requested Suprasena to keep going.

Suprasena adjusted his throat, pitch and continued, "We lost around seventy-thousand soldiers. More than half of the valiant sacrifices belong to Patyadhakshas. May their souls find a rightful place in God's abode. With the help of four eminent soldiers, we have estimated that around one lakh ten thousand Manikuntekan souls have lost their lives. Thanks to the planned implementation of castor-bean arrows. The attack was successful only with the faultless and precise coordination between the foot soldier's, archers and cavalry."

Nodding in agreement with what Suprasena has said, I further added by mentioning the timely appliance of skilful strategy employed by Durvasana and archers which greatly helped in shifting the war mostly in our favour. Suprasena thanking all the dignitaries present, rested after his initial enunciation. I then requested *Acharya Astabhargava* to take forward the deliberation. With a calm, composed spirit, Acharya slowly stood up, appreciating all the valiance demonstrated on day one, squinted at the map and the seated members, crossing his palms backward.

Acharya was one of our most trusted aides and a dear friend to King Chitrasena. Grandfather and Acharya's friendship goes way back to the times of their childhood. One incident that was recalled again and again by grandfather was when he, during his pupillage, was on a horse ride to the forest to fetch some woods for homely needs. Discovering his loneliness and lavish attire, grandfather was caught off-guard and cornered by a group of swindlers pointing knives and hammers at him. Acharya, herding cows nearby, heard large screams and mischievous giggles coming at his ear length from the northeast direction. Without a blink of thought, Acharya rushed and alerted the village elders who came for the grandfather's rescue and successfully whisked away the swindlers. My grandfather's inconsolable wails distinctly evident on his stunned face had drawn Acharya to empathize with him as he offered him long consolations. From that moment forward, their stemmed mutual respect blossomed into a deep-rooted friendship.

After a few years, my grandfather, upon exercising power over the kingdom, travelled four days straight to reach the settlement where Acharya lives. Having spent time with Acharya for a day, grandfather requested the latter to work alongside with him to better the newly built kingdom into a large fraternity where "Equality for all, Justice for all, Prosperity for all, and Education for all" is served to every common man and woman regardless of age, caste, creed or position. Acharya, after giving it a long thought, finally obliged to work alongside his friend. Since then, there was no looking back on the progress of the city and the neighbourhood villages under its rule. Acharya held many notable positions— minister of education and welfare, military strategist, principal lawmaker during his long wisdom of forty-eight years. He pioneered various subsidy schemes at a concession of ninety-two percent to the poor, physically disabled and distressed people who were helpless in affording the basic necessities of survival— food and a place to live.

His formulated slogan, "Right Food, Right Cloth and Right Hut" was included in the top priorities of the governance. In fifteen years after introducing the scheme, with the sizable allocation of the kingdom's earnings had tremendously helped in raising the overall health of the people, reduced the poverty levels, and increased the incorporation of children into education. The steps greatly helped in contributing to more supply of active skilled labour and increased farm production, which subsequently enhanced overall welfare of the kingdom qualitatively.

His studious curiosity and decisive inquisitiveness had made him rationally inquire into every minuscule mystery of nature. He had actively compiled many manuscripts vividly explaining plants, birds, land, spirituality and astronomy. His vast spectrum of knowledge was carefully stored in the private library of the king's chambers, open to only a selected few. On one occasion, I had the chance to witness the aura surrounding Acharya when he was explaining to grandfather about the plausible relationship and symmetry between the behavioural aspects of human beings with the movements of the Sun and the Moon. The logical theories presented baffled as well as convinced our constrained minds.

With his eighty-two years old body, Acharya stood up steadily to offer his perspective about the day-one of war. Our expressions of pride and maturity were transformed into total surrender and submissiveness into paying total attention to the wise, prudent words that he was about to offer. He started by acknowledging the determination and audacity of the dead soldiers that fuelled the entire army's confidence level for the next day. He said, "While we are delegating this meeting, the enemies would be doing the same. They will be planning to take dominance over the decisive day of tomorrow. Seriousness plays a pivotal role in the war but has its own boundaries. Firstly, it should not deprive one person of a proper rest of seven hours. The essential part of a battle is to keep the body, mind and soul active and spirited. It doesn't mean that everyone should sleep at night. The enemy is always unpredictable, most particularly these man-eaters. For he can attack right this moment, or he might be shooting arrows at us even while we are asleep. It is very hard to tell as they paid no heed to the rules of war. So, it is imperative to engage the mildly injured for night duty. Secondly, our understanding of their way of life is vital. As my information goes, I understand their culture is strong as well as fragile. Did anyone notice how the enemies cremated their dead bodies?"

Everyone looked at each other with their puzzled faces and unanimously replied "No."

"Well, they had engaged forty to fifty soldiers to carry all the dead bodies to a nearby hill-top and left it there to be eaten by the scavenging animals. They consider this kind of funeral an offering to the elements of nature." Acharya explained.

The seated warlords were shunned to silence and disbelief, assimilating the information that Acharya was telling. Acharya continued, "But what I rationally deduced from this funeral event was, the enemies have rendered themselves healthy and more active by not shedding a lot of energy. This act helped them to stay active and physically fit for the next day. In contrast, half of our active soldiers were engaged in the funeral activities of our martyrs for one full prahar. God forbid me. I am never against the proper burial of the deceased. But this is a different kind of war altogether and we are facing a different kind of enemy. Isn't it?"

We were all silent to his insight. He was not judging or criticizing us. But, his insights could not be ignored. They would prove to be very handy in tomorrow's face-off.

Acharya continued, "If we by any probability lose, the surviving brothers and the dead, we will both be eaten by the notorious Manikuntekans. I believe I don't need to remind you of their savagery characteristics. At this juncture, we cannot afford even one percent of the flaw."

Durvasana wheezed and asked, "Acharya, considering the minor deviation in activeness compared to the Manikuntekans, how we can possibly overcome this mismatch and instil fear in the enemies?"

With a sly chuckle, pointing at the map with a pointed stick, Acharya rearranged the positions of

Patyadhyakshas, Ashvadhyakshas, and Rathadhyakshas and said, "Radhasaki in all probability will plan his attack by assuming that our infantry will lead the attack from the front as it is usually the most practiced tactics. But tomorrow, we will plan the attack with the cavalry leading from the front, followed by archers and then the foot soldiers." as he rearranged the small white wooden pieces of cavalry, archers and infantry in the described order over the map.

Members around the table, apprehending what Acharya just said, gave a long thought looking over the map on the table. After mulling over for one-fourth of a prahar and jotting down all their queries. Everyone took their seat with Acharya signalling them to raise their queries.

A lean-muscled astute person of average height with a thin-orange shawl suspended from the left forearm containing noticeable bruises on the back of his neck, covered with turmeric-ginger paste to evade the spread of infection from the wound that was endured during the battle, *Kanteshwara*— Rathadhyakshas commander-in-chief, stood up with an unconvinced discernible expression, eyes glued to the map objects and said, "Acharya, with all due respects, I am baffled at your suggested strategy for tomorrow's encounter. Sure, there is no denying that we have allowed some experiments regarding battle positions in the past but never compromised on the sequencing of the three forces in the order of Patyadhyakshas, Ashvadhyakshas, and finally the Rathadhyakshas. Now, you recommend the complete altering of the parallel array sequence. I mean, neither have we heard nor witnessed such a reversed arrangement bearing any results in the past." Burdened with the complex and complicated imagination, tensed and bewildered, chief Kanteshwara continued, "Chariots leading from the front? Pardon me, Acharya. But, the enemies will break the array once they find the weak spot in the unpredictable behaviour of the horses. Once they do, they will breach the entire array and wreak havoc. Our Patyadhyakshas and Ashvadhyakshas will be left with no choice but to retreat leaving behind a mammoth number of casualties."

Everyone around the table exchanged anxious glances except for me. A few years back, I had stumbled upon an intense conversation my grandfather and Acharya were having over a snack of fruits and a cold *Sura* (drink), just before the sun was dimming itself for the day. The drink, a commonly found beverage brewed from the beaten pulp of rice, wheat, barley, grapes and sugarcane. Just then, I made my way into their discussion with their permission. They were profoundly discussing the pros and cons in changing the long-held array orders of the battle forces.

Acharya with a smirk, answered, "I completely understand all your apprehensions. Let me clear all the air of doubt. Firstly, the physical strength of Manikuntekans outweighs our average physical strength. So, by keeping our traditional formation— foot soldiers in the front line of defence. It is fairly obvious to assume that our infantry cannot withhold such a formidable brute force. Agree?"

Everyone nodded in agreement.

"My calculated degree of conjecture is, we will lose six soldiers against one Manikunteka. So, twenty-four thousands of our infantry will be wasted to six thousand Manikuntekans in no time and once there is a breach in our infantry. Measure the time in which they will wreak our archers. Maybe one and a half Prahar hardly. Our Rathadhyakshas will stand very hard for Manikuntekans to break as the strength of our horses and superior weapons our archers carry will be difficult to subjugate. Now, just envisage such a strong and brutal force of Rathadhyakshas (Cavalry) leading from the front with the active support of infantry and archers. Not only will the efficient energy levels of Manikuntekans be doomed to dwindle but also our combined forces will find it easy to vanquish their forces, forcing them to resign, surrender and retreat."

CHAPTER 16

Shri Krishna's edification of Arjuna, 3149 BC

Bowing to Gurudev Veda Vyas in reverence, Krishna said, "Gurudev, your candour and graciousness will always act as a precedent for eons to come. You are the living repository of abundant knowledge, logic, Vedas and Upanishads that will stay alive for thousands of years and act as a principal factor in leading a man's life to the path of divinity and spirituality. I am equally obliged that you have chosen me to pass on whatever little knowledge I have about the nuances of austerity."

Blessing Krishna with a warm smile, Vyas Maharshi said, "My blessings are always with you, *Dinabandhu* (other name of Krishna)."

As time rowed forward, the initial formal discussion which had started as a jest, took a wild turn into an intellectual debate, slowly pulling the likes and presence of everyone under the large palm tree, where the scholarly discussion is being held. Slowly, one by one in this order of Yudhishthira, Gurudev Veda Vyas, Draupadi, Ghatotkacha, Hidimbi, Sahadeva and few more helpers spectated the most breath-taking and enriching debate that had been carrying on for two prahars.

With a sly smile playing on his thin lips, Krishna said, "*Partha* (other name of Arjuna), to evoke Shiva's energy with tenacious meditation and resilient single-mindedness, remember you must not cause hurt in any way to the primary resource of your life— your body. You must not hurt it either from thirst or hunger. Only then will your body be able to assist your mind and spirit in achieving your spiritual objective.

Avinashi tu tad viddhi

Yena sarvam idam tatam

Vinasam avyayasyasya

Na kascit kartum arhati

O' *Yogi* (learned one)! Remember. Your formidable body encapsulates your celestial spirit. Know that the incorporeal self or the soul is indestructible. It permeates the entire universe as a single unit of energy. It is thus your mind or thoughts clouded by the dusted ideas and veils of unfulfilled desires compelling you to stay blind from witnessing or realizing your inner consciousness of oneness."

"O' *Purushottama Krishna*, then why do many yogi's neglect and subject their bodies to extremes levels of torture to please God and yet they succeed?" enquired Arjuna.

With a slight chuckle, while shaking his head, Krishna said, "

Na karmanam anarambhan

Naiskarmyam puruso snute

Naca sanyasanad

Eva siddhim samadhi gacchati

Arjuna, without the onset of sublime self-awareness or the touch of transcendent consciousness, neither renunciation nor the abstinence from daily orderly life can lead a man into the path of perfection. And when a man decides to torment one's own body and when a man strongly believes that suppressing and withholding the excruciating pain will lead into pleasing the almighty. Then every predator and the being-hunted animal will ultimately reach God, for there is none that is more eligible to reach the pinnacle of awareness than an animal who is subjected to intense distress and pain, before they die if that logic stands correct. And the man carrying a line of thought of such is bound to be clinging to a various set of desires, albeit in a different form. Sure, their cravings will be fulfilled by the almighty. But that does not send the idea that they were freed from the clutches of appetite for desires. The whole purpose of meditation is to dissolve oneself into the universal energy and gain salvation from never-ending desires."

"Isn't my austerity guided by the desire to acquire powerful Pashupatastra?" Arjuna reverted.

"To start with, yes. You are guided by the desire to acquire possession." said Krishna, slowly moving to his right, with his hands clasped backward and continued,"

Yas tv indriyani

Manasa niyamyarabhate 'rjuna

Karmendriyaih karma-yogam

Asaktah sa visisyate

As you progress with the meditation with each passing day, your conscious self is caught in the spider web of attachment, expectations, sensual pleasures coupled with never-ending desires. In those testing moments, your single-mindedness and unflinching devotion towards *Lord Pasupati* will decide whether your desires will act as a mere catalyst in transforming you to a *Sidhi— an attained soul* or a driving force compelling you to greed more and more."

"What exactly should be my motive then?" queried Arjuna confusingly.

"The very purpose and delight of meditation is to remove every attached ambiguity and to be devoid of any motives, expectations and varied desires. To put it clearly, your intake and exhalation of breath carries the entire burden of your body, not your thoughts. But the average human being carries the misconception that thoughts guide the spirit. It's the breath that guides your senses into a specific set of emotions of varying frequencies. Your meditation will transform your agitated breath into a natural, calm flowing breath. In turn, your entire spectrum of senses, thoughts, and whims will be centralized around the energy of the breath. Then and only then, Arjuna, will you be called

114

a *Siddha*, an awakened soul." replied Krishna, taking a deep breath with closed eyes. He requested Vyas Maharshi to brief about prerequisite rituals to be carried before austerity.

CHAPTER 17

Homecoming—

The surviving army, animals, medical staff and everyone started marching towards the kingdom. Exuberance flooded on the cheering faces of many. Melancholy drenched itself in the psyches of many mourning the losses of their near and dear ones. Some beating their drums, some singing in unison. Amidst the exhausted horses with their endless neighs, we were marching to our homes celebrating the victory of truth over evil and mourning the departure of noble souls.

I could recognize the tiredness seeping into the warriors and the elated glow on many of my compatriots. It was quite evident from their faces that they were eager to fondle with the winds of the home side, embrace into the arms of their loved one. *O' I miss the nonsensical bursting cackles of my son, I miss the affectionate caressing of my wife, I miss the very presence of my mother, the gust of the breeze, the bustling's of the busy city, the games, the dramatic plays played in the dedicated arena, the aroma of the plantations and a pleasant pleasing swim along the calming river. Huh!*

By the onset of the third sunset, we had started ourselves for home—*our home*. Soldiers hand in hand with compatriots, singing and reminiscing about the winning, we started towards our abiding home. I always felt that mere appreciations or bestowing of gifts were no match of the devoutness and commitment of the medical servicemen. Even when the war was over, even when the bloodthirsty violence had ended, there was no vacation for the labour put out by the medical team. When everyone was jolly and dancing to the victory, when everyone breathed a sigh of relief from the barbaric Manikuntekans, I was compelled not to ignore the efforts of the medical servicemen, carrying the injured in hundreds in number with all the precautions and without any hindrance to their continuous medical care. Their sole motive, it seemed and was evident from the unselfish act of theirs, was to keep the life alive and honour the life given.

It is pertinent to mention, of one instance, after the verdict of war, one member of our medical team couldn't help but notice a gravely injured Manikunteka, with one limb hanging half-cut, screaming in extreme pain, with parched tears soaking in his own blood. Without a second thought, he went straight up to him and offered the combination of some herbal painkillers. He then requested Durvasana to pass on calm painless death to the person, as there was no chance of his survival. Such a selfless act, carrying no room for expectations or pleasures was theirs.

Radhasaki. Hm! It was worth reminiscing the motionless expression and sad grimace on the face of Radhasaki. His contorted eyes, unable to withstand or fathom the taintless defeat, dawn upon his vast formidable undefeatable force. His eyes constantly moving hitherto left to right, in quick succession to the laid down bodies of his fellow Manikuntekans, the same bodies that were violently dancing to the tunes of vengeance a day prior, he reckoned.

I called Suprasena, who was supervising the safe voyage of the people back to the kingdom. I screamed and signalled for him again but he was deeply focussed on examining the proper storage of the weapons. However, he finally caught hold of my cry and responded with a waving hand.

Suprasena understands my anguish and we share the same emotions about the war. Neither we celebrate the positive outcome of the war, nor do we congratulate each other, for we know, even the war won has many casualties to cremate, many memories to bury and forcing many families into a state of gloominess. Celebrating a war to us seemed to be a pointless mockery of the departed souls. It doesn't mean that I go against the ones celebrating the victory. I reciprocate every congratulatory message that I receive with a tender "Congratulations" in return. And I compel no one from celebrating, as I feel it is equally their deserving right to celebrate and make merry.

Suprasena approached me with a quick smirk, "What happened?" and continued, "As much as one-third of our weapons and armoury has been damaged. We have collected almost four by fifth, including the damaged weaponry and the rest will be completed, I think in half a prahar mostly." fixing a taunting gaze at me "How can

I be of help? Your highhhhhhh—ness." Suprasena said in jest, mocking me.

Locking Suprasena in my arms from behind "Now I suppose, the rumour circulating in our tax department is no more a rumour but a plain fact."

"What rumour?" Suprasena inquired curiously, still trying very hard to break free from my iron hold.

"That you are born with a cross-over of a man and a hideous boar." And we both burst into laughter.

Witnessing the elation dancing on the exhausted faces, all I could do was thank Acharya for devising such an inconceivable and faultless strategy for our day two of battle. I must also thank Durvasana, for his skilful focussed demeanour and tactful execution of strategy without any room for error. In roughly two prahars, we have been able to bring the war into our domitable hold with the bare minimum loss of combatants. Radhasaki's forces were left with no option but to surrender and retreat. Many managed to run away realising the futility of their efforts before our bravery and master plan. Such was the tenacious hold we had upon them.

But, in our war meeting the previous night, on a voting decisiveness of five to four we decided not to recuperate and rescue the injured horses back to the kingdom as the majority felt that would involve much of the force and it would cost enormous resources. But, the agonizing whining's of the gravely mutilated horses, the sight of their dislodged limbs, the dripping pile of blood-dried and sun-soaked large dilated oval eyes conveying a thousand muted dreary words that had sent shuddering chills to my nerves and ruptured my soul into dark tears. Noticing my disoriented psyche, Suprasena said in a consoling and dreaded tone, "We are helpless, Babru."

"Huh!" I murmured.

My mind went off hastily to search for the largely built black dog. *There it is, with its thirty-two-inch dark body, sniffing every damn thing that's on its way.* I quickly grabbed it by force and gave soothing strokes on its neck. The dog stretched its neck upwards, giving way for my strokes. Obviously, the dog seemed to enjoy the tickles of my fingers.

"So, what are your plans with this dog? Are you planning to turn over the dog to the army overseeing the security of our boundary? By the looks of its humongous size and weight, sure it will scare the onlookers." Suprasena asked, not taking his eyes off the dog.

Five of my best men capped the berserk dog with large iron chains and wrapped it around its stout neck. It took them a hefty time to contain the monster. I can discern the troubled look soaking in Radhasaki's face, not out of fear for his own life, not out of concern for his fellow men. But, his troubled disquietness tended towards the safety of the dog. The dog that he adored more than his own life. Shocked at the unfurling rarity, I ordered the fellow men to stop bashing the dog. That moment, I had elicited the attention of Radhasaki to my words. Forthwith, I offered the choice to Radhasaki, "Either I spare your life or the dog's? You have got a quick snap of time."

Radhasaki, without any delay and hesitation replied, "Spare the dog's life and promise me that you will look after her. She is a great girl."

I stared into the bereaved eyes of the dog and then moved to Radhasaki and said, "You have my word of honour." My promise invoked a delicate smile on Radhasaki's face and with a slightly bent posture, I severed the head of Radhasaki with a single blow from my blood-stained blade.

I replied to Suprasena, keeping my eyes glued to the dog, "She will be in my care."

"Are you sure of what you are saying? From the looks of it, Rasikri and Aitreya will feel the burden of this beastly dog. They might disagree with you on this." said Suprasena cautiously.

"Foremost, stop addressing it as a beast. Her name is *Manvi*." And for your knowledge, "Manvi is part of the family and it's quite natural for the family to have disagreements but never hatred towards each other."

Grinning at Suprasena, I continued, "Now let's have some delicious food that our boys have been cooking. I have been craving this for a long time now."

Four days of intermittent travel, contrasting temperatures ranging from extreme shivering cold to an apogee of torrid heat waves exhausted the bodies and anima of soldiers. I could see the weakening efficacy, yet the resolution to reach in the arms of their dear home had kept them moving and moving. Every possible effort had been tried to engage the soldiers. A touch of music, some joyous dances, and all forms of entertainment, yet the indulgences proved to be a futile exercise in lifting their spirits.

En route, while passing through a narrow hilly terrain, the heavy gush of wind and the slippery path proved fatal to the weakened, mildly injured and some unfortunate people. Apart from being helpless, what whipped our souls was to remain as a mere spectator to hundreds of unanticipated deaths materializing right in front of our eyes. The bodies collapsed into the deep trenches of ridges like falling rocks. Their heavy clamoured wails of "Help me" echoed and echoed in our deaf minds. Even if we had the gutsy intention of rescuing the lain bodies, our inability and near-impossible rescue mission fractured our tormented soul. *The thought of the last Vedic rites, the deceased rightfully deserved but didn't gain as they were not performed. The thought of the surviving family members not catching the last glimpse of their fathers, brothers and sons nearly destroyed the very purpose of our already dead lives.*

The horrors and the massacre this ruinous war compelled us to witness sometimes forces us to realize the truer inner authentic self of ours, which has been long suppressed— *an inhuman barbarian, an inhuman barbarian is what we are.* I always believed in my core, *War never wins, nor does it bring peace. The only thing the war is best at performing is artfully destroy lives and create ruins for generations to mourn.*

We thrivingly managed to survive the horror-filled voyage. We previously had not endured any difficulties in crossing the *Dhanush* Mountains. But, this time the harsh climate had taken a toll on many lives during the passage. We decided to make a short sojourn, rejuvenate ourselves and start over again.

The smell of the emanating breeze, the incense of the river *Meghna's* moisture in the air caught up with our nostrils. I cannot describe the jubilance dancing in the air and the cheering faces that are infected with the aroma of delight. The joy of dance, the beating of drums and high spirits resumed in our resilient camp. Even I cannot stop myself from admiring the beauty of embracing our nativity.

Usually, it would take one and a half prahar to cross the river Meghna and reach the city. But, witnessing the raised spirits among the camp, we expected the journey would be completed in one prahar.

The beatings of my heart reached a new pace as that of a horse. The panic and the stress shook my nerves, disabling me from inhaling like a normal person. I looked for Suprasena and realised he was nowhere to be found. I looked for Durvasana and he was busy managing the transitions. Manvi stood there beside me with its tongue laid out and I fell into her embrace, stroking her hair and neck and in those moments, in that crack of time, I couldn't control my overjoyed tears— my tears of fulfilment, tears of my promise of keeping their families safe and I sobbed inconsolably.

When everyone was jeering, jumping recklessly, throwing objects and their clothes into the air when the sound of a large semi-circle trumpet was continuously being played far-off east near the wooden entrance gate. Conch shells followed the trumpet from the city entrance gate and the beating of our drums grew louder and louder in response. The sight and the sound felt surreal, evoking the quintessence of emotions.

The wild running of belonging families from both sides, their long-held embrace, the blissful tears aroused from their meeting along with the gloominess of many children and women intensifying with each passing moment as they were helpless to meet their dear ones. One team, specially designated for human relations, was approaching the distressed families, one by one to inform them of their family member's demise during the war.

Amidst all the chaotic noises, amongst all the grieving individuals and delighted family members, I saw a petite child figure emerging from the crowd, drawing closer and closer. With the happening sunset, I could only see the shadow overpowering the little body. With each step closing towards me, the fascinating memories struck my subconscious mind into realizing the charming, dazzling child was my son *Aitreya*— my breath, and my life.

The embrace, long-held embrace. The cracking words of *father, father, father* flying in the air. The touch of the bubbly cheeks when kissed, the soft little hands wrapped around my back, the chuckles of him when I tickled his belly. *O' God, in those moments of euphoria, my long anguish, my oppressive pains, the wails of my destitute soul, every tremor of this bloodshed had subsided and peace descended over my empty soul.*

And, finally, we were home.

CHAPTER 18

The test of transcendence—

"Your words have evoked the muted gravels of the dormant spirit into the trance of wisdom and path to awakening. I bow to your acumen, Krishna." said Vedvyas graciously and continued, "Arjuna now that you have gained knowledge about the fruitfulness of meditation from Krishna. Allow me to pass on the technicalities involved in the ascetic practice."

"What more could I ask for, Gurudeva. I am being guided by two God-like personas. I am truly blessed, Gurudeva." said Arjuna, folding his hands with his closed eyes.

"Arjuna. The meditation practice consists of three main stages— the body, the mind and the spirit. It is indispensable that the body is always taken care of in terms of its health and nutrition, just as Krishna elucidated. Just remember, the body ignored is the equilibrium perturbed. So, after you perform the *Surya-namaskara* with the first light, consume the paste of *Tulasi* in combination with honey. It will rejuvenate your body and prepare your mind to peacefully practice meditation. Then, carve a palm-sized *Shivalinga* from red-clay and place it in the east corner of the cave. Offer prayers to the eternal Lord Shiva and with an erect spine seated in Padmasana with *Gyan Mudra*, start meditating on 'Om'. Thereafter, in every two prahars, sustain your body with adequate quantities of plant and little animal food with sufficient hydration that is needed for the body. Remember, don't spend too much energy and thoughts on nourishment. Excessive care for body nutrition can also destroy your sanctity of meditation. Secondly, *the mind*. The mind, Arjuna, is the clever enchantress injecting your consciousness with an appetite for lavishness, craving for power and hunger and thirst for extravagance. It directs you to act otherwise with compelling logical arguments the mind provides. Always remember, it succumbs you into an artful trap to disrupt the austerity. For the mind to be held in control, suppression is never the answer. *Sakshi* (witness). Mere witnessing the spider web of thoughts will bring you to the path of omniscience and will dissipate the mind's deceptive energy." That being said, Veda Vyas continued, "Let me quote a verse from *Shwetashvatara Upanishad*

Eko devam: Sarvabhuteshu gud:

Sarvavyapi sarvabhuthantharathma |

Karmadhyaksha: sarvabhutadivas:

Sakshi cheta kevalo nirgunasch | |

God, even when he is called by many with countless names. That God is one. For he is both formless and celestial. He dwells in the innermost being of beings. He endures all the pains and pleasures, yet he is affected by none. He administers and governs all thoughts, yet he experiences none. He is the giant witness to all the actions. He is the spirited witness to all the dynamism. Yet he is affected by none. Therefore, O' *Phalguna!* (Another name of Arjuna as he was born in the third or fourth month of year as per Gregorian calendar) Try becoming the *Sakshi* of all your actions and thoughts. Once you attain the witnessing, you will unbecome from the becoming. You will detach from the acquired attachments, and you will be freed from all the bonds and expectations, and you will be a pure *Sakshi*. Lastly, your imperishable spirit will be illuminated both with the active chanting of *Om* and with the total witnessing of your wholeness."

Deeply engrossed in the words of Guru Veda Vyas, Arjuna asked, "In what time or in what approximate years can I expect Lord Shiva's presence and blessings, Gurudev?"

"Arjuna. That can only be ascertained by the tranquillity of your meditation. It may well be six months or may extend to thirty years. It solely depends on the realization of your immaculate light encapsulated in the depths of your spirited soul." said Gurudeva.

Eight straight months of intense meditation, four prahars every day. With every tiny protocol followed enumerated by Krishna and Gurudeva Veda Vyas. Arjuna's vital *Atman* (soul) was transcending beyond thoughts and buoyant attachments. In the initial period of austerity, during the times of sustaining basic needs, Arjuna yearned for the presence of his dear ones and momentarily missed them. But, that sense of longing drifted into a state of nullity, giving way for the single-mindedness as the austerity progressed. Even the echoing of the silence was muted, and he became *the silence*.

One fine day, when he was in pursuit of a wild boar, in the deserted forest land, holding the heavy bow into the sky. Adjusting the angle with the calculated stretch of the arrow and bow string, just when he was certain that the arrow would pierce into the running boar at a specific speed. Arjuna heard an echoing shout at him which told him to halt the release of the arrow.

Arjuna was dismayed at the reverberating voice that advanced through the camel-shaped mountains. The echoing voice colliding with every cold wind particle hustled through the giant colossal trees and its leaves. His curiosity about the originator of the sound was baffling him. One more time, with more vigour in its pitch, it reached his ear, "The boar belongs to me, as I laid my eyes and aimed at it first." The assertion of ownership infuriated and provoked the sensibility of Arjuna.

Without paying attention to the warning, Arjuna released the arrow piercing right into the body of the boar, which also received a series of arrows from the other side, instantly ebbing the life from the boar. Finally, Arjuna beheld the man appearing to be a mountaineer, who was claiming the ownership of the boar.

Arjuna, in an assuring tone, said, "O' *Kirata*! O' mountaineer! I see no business of you in this deserted forest enveloped in the mountains. You, along with your lady, I command you to return to the place that you have come from without the boar. As you can clearly see, my arrow laid down its body to the ground first."

Smiling to himself, the tiger skin drooping over his left shoulder covering the upper chest, a loincloth hanging down the waist, a small arrow pricking through the knotted hair on the head, Kirata looked at his wife and back at Arjuna and clamoured, "O' warrior! You look soft, you look weak and you don't seem fit for staying in the mountains. These are not relatable to your home. Yet, you have dared to order me to vanish from my dwelling. I have lived the air that you are breathing and breathed the mountains, the forest and the cold waves and the riverbeds. And you dare tell me to leave. Now, I command you to leave my place, leave my hunt before I terrorize you with arrows."

Furiousness crept into Arjuna's senses at the adamance of the Kirata. Outraged at the stubbornness and boldness, Arjuna said, "You dare challenge the son of lighting, the rightful grantee of *Guru Dronacharya's* wisdom and a valiant Pandava. Now, I will warn you for the last time to relinquish the land that you are presently standing, else I will be compelled to declare combat over your petty life. Give a wise thought about it." growling at Kirata, Arjuna was sharpening his arrow heads, getting himself prepared for the confrontation.

CHAPTER 19

The aroma of own abode—

I introduced Manvi to Aitreya. In the beginning, Aitreya was a little frightened to advance towards Manvi. Noticing the hugely built, almost four times his body, Aitreya enquired, "*Baba* (father), this dog looks exactly like the recently born baby elephant except for the large tongue and continuous barks." "Hehe," chuckled Aitreya with his soft rounded face, his broken teeth visible.

"The last time I saw you, you were full of teeth. What happened to the missing middle one?" I teasingly enquired, with a small pinch to his belly.

"Mother said, each missing tooth can be glimpsed during the night in the sparkling stars." looking up in the evening sun, Aitreya continued, "I can show you where my tooth is? When the night approaches and becomes silent."

"Hm, let's see how your tooth shines in the night." I tickled again, with a smile playing on my lips that was long concealed.

"Please, Baba, stop with the tickling." Aitreya requested me while laughing out loud and gasping for breath with each tickle.

"Now, just the way I tickled you, you can rub Manvi's body and tickle it in the neck." I instructed Aitreya.

I grabbed his hand and proceeded towards Manvi, where she was sitting silently, ogling here and there. I could tell by the looks in her eyes that she was terribly missing the smell, pampering and the sight of Radhasaki.

Aitreya took little time, going forth and back and finally they were acquainted and became friends together. "Baba, I like her. Can we keep the dog with us?" Aitreya enquired while playing with Manvi.

"She has come to stay with us forever. And her name is Manvi, your dear sister." Finally marvelling at the happy faces of both Manvi and Aitreya, I turned to look at every nook and corner frantically searched in anticipation and desperation for the sight of my dear soul.

Suprasena, out of the blue, dabbed me from behind and shouted "Aitreyaaaaaa" and moved towards my son.

"Unccccccccle......" Aitreya jumped into the arms of Suprasena and went on asking questions about the war and enemies.

Suprasena, as was his style, went on explaining less of the truth and more of exaggerated heroism about him and all about himself. How he had managed to sword fight eighty people at once. How he called an eagle to help him in the war and all his wild imaginations, none of which was true even remotely.

Utter bullshit I thought.

Noticing my restlessness, Suprasena shouted in a large tone, "Rasikri is waiting for you."

"Where?" I enthusiastically asked.

He turned to Aitreya, after teasingly passing a warm smile at me, "The place where you both used to meet secretly, *Kutasha.*"

I immediately bustled to the place that is close to my heart and soul, the place that my mother gifted me, built it herself personally for me when I was barely walking. I still remember her words that she said when I was an adolescent, "Babru, consider this place as your learning centre. Here and only here. The cow and its calves, the variety of birds and its movements, the flock of sheep, and the wide diversity of trees and saplings will henceforth be your teachers."

She quickly fathomed my confused look, smiled and continued, "These speechless animals, these trees and the birds will play a decisive role in harnessing your personality. From now on, you will be tasked with taking care of these animals and trees. It's your responsibility to pay attention to, witness and nurture this place into a pulsating land. You will understand as time progresses the pivotal role this garden has played in your life. This greenfield will henceforth be called *Kutasha*— seeking nature."

I couldn't understand her words then, but as time progressed with the moments spent rearing the cows and sheep or watering the saplings or feeding the birds. The acts have given me a sense of belongingness and a spirited awakening. My myriad detached thoughts submerged into oblivion, and I felt the same perpetual energy pulsating both in trees and me, with the animals and myself. The experience was something indescribable, like our energies were bridged together into oneness.

During one such time, where I lost myself into the pearls of the ethereal universe was being part of nature's magical event when a mother cow was giving birth to a calf. I was fourteen then. *O' Lord Shiva! Omkara Nityasundara Sadashiva! I feel blessed to witness such enchanting procreation.* I stood there as still as a motionless mountain. My eyes bulged out and my jaw dropped down, my sedated blood rushed like a giant swelling of the river, witnessing the joyful pain the mother was enduring. The restlessness seeping into her vibrating body, the restless moorings of the cow and the water bag slowly appearing from *Yoni* (Vulva)— the source of creation. My mother stiffened her hands on my shoulder, assuring me quietly of fineness. There, at that moment, the water bag bulged, the wails of the mother grew louder with the clear visibility of red veins over her body. The water bag broke and a small head with a large oval-eyed calf emerged and then the chest and the whole body fell on the ground in a flash. I was transfixed at the unfolding divineness. Those large oval eyes twinkling, the weak body on the ground receiving the first light of the Sun, the first sniff of the wind and

134

the first warmth of a mother. At that moment, a whole lot of me was metamorphosed into a new individual.

I breathed in as I staggered myself to the garden slowly as lull as a child. At long last, there she was— seated on an oval, shiny rock, left leg resting over the right. Butterfly-like soft dark hands pleasantly placed over the legs with the left palm over the right one. Head turned to the lumpsy sheep, her knotted hair as thick and large as an elephant trunk brooding over the ground. She hadn't changed a bit except for a few grey hairs mildly visible. I reckon the growth is due to the heavy chattering inside her mind while I am gone and away.

I stood there muted and unmoved, reminiscing the sight of her. The subtle presence of her effulgent beauty injected a tiny capsule of a charismatic spell of love into my vacant soul. She grasped my presence and gently turned towards me. Her supple oval eyes pierced my heart, her soft-lined lips chiding my conscience. I was momentarily paralyzed. The absurd noises around me evaporated into thin dusky air. So many words were exchanged; so much was said without a word uttered between the two of us, but just by looking at each other. She stood up and with that exerted force, a small tear collided with the earth. I could see her tears bundling up with emotions of days and lengths of missing my presence, long awaiting for my safe arrival. Sleepless nights spent worrying for my safety and my life. As we stood there transfixed in each other. I gently smiled. She reverted with squeezed eyebrows and a hushed smile. I tenderly moved to her, held her hand, and assured her, "I am with you now, Rasikri."

"The last time I saw Aitreya, he was running towards you. Did you meet him?" asked Rasikri.

"Oh. Yes!"

"Then where is he?"

"He is with Suprasena and he has got a new sister, Manvi. I guess he will have less time for us from now on." I chuckled.

"What's that sarcastic smile? Is she that sweet and adorable that my love towards my son will be small-scaled?" She teasingly enquired while gently punching my shoulder with her hand.

"Maybe, yes. Manvi could move mountains with her heart-warming love and affection. You will see."

The bustling market was celebrating our victory over the draconian barbarians— there were vibed greetings, congratulating and blessing me, when we were on my way to our home. Many were staging war performances with counterfeit swords available in the market. I couldn't help but enjoy the joyful atmosphere of today. Many women were seen throwing flowers upon the soldiers and over me from the rooftop.

"Oh! I must admit. You have got a good amount of lady followers." Rasikri sarcastically whispered to me.

"I can sense envy flying in the air. Now I realize whose it was." I jovially commented at Rasikri.

The brimming smiles and their wide dilated eyes gave pleasure and contention for the heroic sacrifices that were laid during the war.

Mother and Rasikri had arranged a dinner celebration for the entire kingdom on account of the warrior's victory and safe return preceded by a long day of prayer for the departed souls.

There she is. Luminous and beautiful as always. I touched my mother's feet in reverence and asked for her blessings. She benevolently raised me and kissed my forehead. Her skin was dropping all suppleness, wrinkles running under her eyes, yet her eyes were illumining with each passing day, blossoming and radiating. She was neither elated nor troubled with the outcome of the war. Her tranquil eyes reflected the nature of her soul— *Illumined, awakened and at ease.*

In the hall of the audience, I exchanged warm greetings with the dignitaries of the kingdom. I could also see the faces seated across the halls, raising their hands, with broad smiles at our return with victory. Those were the same people who once used to pass scornful comments about the absurdity of my birth and my mother's sanctity.

I moved to look at my mother and her hands gestured at me with stretch in her facial muscles, "What happened?"

I simply smiled and nodded, "Nothing."

CHAPTER 20

Beholding the omniscient—

Crushed rocks were crumbling on the ground, shredded trees spread all over the land, baffled and dazed forest animals were running hitherto due to the frightening plague of menace unveiled with the relentless and ferocious clash between Arjuna and Kirata. It had been ongoing for nine days. The slaughtered boar was long abandoned and forgotten. Now the battle was not about the possession of the boar but the clash of two enormous unyielding egos.

Eventually, after realizing the arrows numbered in thousands in the quiver were dwindling to depletion, Arjuna wondered, *even the bravest of warriors and the Gods of war cannot withstand the powerful arrows of mine. Who possibly can this half-naked forest dweller be? Challenging my very potential? My powerful arrows have proved to be futile. The bestowed arrows and mantras from the lord of five elements of Nature— earth, water, fire, wind, and space too are wasted. Who possibly can this man be? Still, energy-filled and unaffected and standing straight like a Himalayan Mountain.* Arjuna wondered, tired of utilizing all the powerful weapons on the Kirata.

Arjuna decided to attack the Kirata with the steel sword. He lanced upon Kirata swinging the sword, only to realize after half a day of sword scuffle that the Kirata was far more exceptional in handling the sword than expected. The manner and ease with which he dodged Arjuna's skilful hooked strikes were beyond phenomenal. It was something Arjuna had never witnessed.

When every attack was proving to be futile, Arjuna incensed with fury, dogged at Kirata, head on head combat, with bare hands. Mustering up all the strength, Arjuna hurled heavy rocks and large trees only to be deflected and fended off by the Kirata. The stumbling rocks and trees perturbed the wild animals, compelling them to hide and run for survival.

The surging ego of Arjuna was peaked with the callous ridicule of his skills and strength by Kirata's display of warrior skills. He rowed forward and started to pound punches after punches with no effect to be inflicted upon the Kirata. But, the right-fisted punch of the Kirata at Arjuna's chest trembled and dismissed Arjuna to nine feet away. Arjuna felt the heavy punch to his ribs and found the difficulty in squeezing the breath. He stood knocked to the ground in the knees.

That very wink of the moment, when Arjuna was regaining the strength to attack again, he beheld the purple-coloured *Datura flower* beaded around the Kirata's neck. He couldn't believe his senses of what he was witnessing. The flowers without a mark were undoubtedly offered by himself to the Shivalinga every morning before resuming to the long duration of meditation. The flowers were nowhere to be found except in the caves that he was meditating as Gurudev Vyas had instructed.

Few moments of quietening of Arjuna's mind, thoughts as calm as a serene flowing river, the petals of blindness altogether were abolished with the dawn of realization. The longing soul ruptured into a flood of tears, the tears of remorse and of bliss. Arjuna, the mightiest warrior of the Bharatkanda, plunged to the feet of Kirata, with his tears cleansing the Kirata's feet and pleading for forgiveness for his ranting ignorance. *The unconquered Kirata is none other than Lord Shiva himself, descending to the mortal earth to bless and transcend Arjuna.*

Kirata and his Ardhangi (wife) raised Arjuna and with a gracious smile and blessed him and said, "In the seven worlds of the eternal universe, neither mortal nor immortal, neither God nor a demon stood a chance to survive this long in a fight with me." A huge four feet venomous *Naga Snake* crawled to the neck of Kirata by coiling three times, wheeling from the foot of the body reaching gently to the nape of the neck.

The calm, unperturbed vibrancy, the blazing glistering light emanating between Kirata's eyes with the long-stranded hair, hung unto the knees. Beholding the celestial form and not able to withstand the slithering guiltiness, Arjuna lamented without looking into the beholden and cried, "O' *Sadashiva! Mrityunjaya* (vanquisher of death)! I failed to see your presence because of my arrogant eyes. How do I forgive myself for the greatest sin that I perpetrated? The ascetics and Danavas, Gods and the Rakshasas, Brahmin and the underprivileged, every living soul earns to least get a glimpse of your celestial self in their life. Here I am, a condemned soul, hurling poisonous arrows at you, flinging my sword to kill you. Launching rocks, trees, and fists at you. I don't earn a living, my Lord. Please behead me, *Bhoothanatha* (Lord of the spirits). Behead me."

The wretched demonic creatures covered in smear ashes, carrying the skull pieces of different animals, with some demons without a limb attached to the upper body and some with their tongues touching their chest, heavy tusked elephants and deer's started mounting behind Lord Shiva, taking solace under his divine presence.

With a calming tone, Lord Shiva said, "Speak no more, Arjuna. Your actions have demonstrated your vigour and agility, leaving no room for error or foul play. I was pleased with your actions towards devotion and combat. Here, I bestow you with *Pashupatastra* at your disposal."

"I am blessed, *Paramajyoti Bholenatha* (illumined Lord)! I am truly blessed that I beheld your elegance."

Lord Shiva continued, "The weapon can only be discharged through awakeness, single-mindedness and with purified spirit. The states to which you are rightly entitled, Arjuna. This weapon shall not be used by a weak mind or with a selfish motive. The weapon, if and when invoked, will destroy every living soul and wipe out the entire existence into dust. Even I cannot stop it."

CHAPTER 21

The forging of tenacious spirits—

My mother, her toughness was as strong as a mammoth mountain able to withstand the draconian oceanic waves, her empathetic love showered affection on every being without a hint of discrimination, was as a result of years of detestable remarks, she had to endure since my birth.

People called her a shameful loathable wench. Her walk along the market was a nightmare. Her horse riding among the crowded place was considered a sinful act. Many people fled the place she had set foot on. Women shut their doors at the very sight of her and the uncouth young lad's derisive comments about my mother's secret lover and comments about my sinful birth without the sanctity of marriage had shattered my mother's core of the soul into irreparable damage. There was never a day where her mind was squeezing her lone body so hard to shed the last tear. Countless days were spent without the body being fed with the right amount of food.

My grandfather was unable to find solace by looking at his lone daughter and witnessing the agony of his only child. He couldn't help but look for an escape by going hunting for the deer's in the forest to divert his mind, unable to see the torment and misery his daughter was going through.

I had my fair share of slandering and abuse. Wherever I went, I was asked by my friends, elders or any scoundrels looking for fun. I was their soft target and their object of entertainment. Being at a tender age, I couldn't answer nor comprehend the questions I was being asked, "Who is my father? What does my mother do when she is alone? Am I born out of heaven or the skies? Why is my mother not being seen these days? Why can't my mother bear children with one of them?"

From the moment I opened my eyes and breathed in the air, all I knew of was my mother and her nurturing and her love. Never had I felt the need of a father nor did I understand his rightful role in my life until I received my fair share of bullying and slandering. In those moments of scathing events, I either hid or ran. Once, I ran and hurriedly ran to my mother and narrated the whole incident to her. All I could notice was her teary dried eyes at her knowing that I was being called a "Bastard son." Broken bangles at the heavy banging of her head with her hands, the bitterness of pain sweeping over her stained hands, but never did she answer my repetitive question "Who is my father?"

I got used to being called a "bastard" by sections of society. *Whether during playing a game with the kids or going to the temple for prayer or fetching some vegetables. The result was always the same. I was always mocked with a hateful look and scornful hurling of bastard and a bastard son.*

Defeated and aggrieved, I rushed to my grandfather, sobbing my lungs out to demand the answers about my sinful birth— *that the society brands my birth as "a sinful birth"*. Heartbroken and dejected, my grandfather grieved over and over, and consoled me that the only mistake he regrets making was agreeing to the demands put out by my nameless father to perform the marriage rituals in private without the knowledge of the third world. That haste decision haunts him every time he looks at my wailing and distraught mother.

"Least, tell me his name, grandfather. I deserve at least that minimum information being his son." I pleaded sobbingly.

Helpless and sorrow-filled, he said, "Sorry, Babru. Only your father is entitled to answer that." He rubbed my head and moved away. *I thought one day, he had to. That day, my spine-less father must face the reflection of himself. That day he has to look straight into my eyes and answer my deeply suppressed anguish.*

More than the woeful thoughts about my birth-giving father, more than my deplorable state of mind, I was worried about my mother and her continued denial of life. Tired and petrified of facing the crowd or even a living being, she forced herself into the pitch-black hugely built room for two long years. The food was placed at the doorsteps by the caretakers. Grandfather's painful efforts to speak to her and console her, proved futile. Her only communion with the outside world was through me. I apprised her of my growing, outside gossip, the changes that happened in the city, etc. My countless pleas to her to come to the outside too meted with the same result.

One sunny morning, when my grandfather was on a hunt, he happened to know about Guru Lespakamanya and his location from some forest dwellers. The next morning, he went to his small hut, in hopes he would cure his daughter's state of mind. The hut was filled with roaming peacocks and leopards in the garden. The hut was open as there was no door. Grandfather proceeded into the hut that was made of bamboo and saw Guru Lespakamanya deep in meditation. His long white-haired beard, half-closed upward-directed eyes bolted my grandfather's senses. He waited there for three prahars, yet the yogi didn't break the *Samadhi* (meditative trance). He went there for six straight days, only to sit in his presence and patiently wait for the yogi (Sage) to open his eyes. But every time, it was the same routine— walking to the hut, dancing peacocks, leopards resting or moving here and there, the ducks moving in a small pond nearby. On the sixth day, Gurudev Lespakamanya opened his eyes and instructed my grandfather, in a calm tone, to take him to his daughter. My grandfather was spellbound. No one other than a few knew about his daughter's self-confinement. Neither did the yogi leave the hut nor did anyone come to the hut because every day he was the only one visiting the yogi. My grandfather, shocked and speechless beyond comprehension, said in broken words, "Yes, Gurudev. As you command."

I remember the day as fresh as today, going through the paintings hung in the room, the room my mother confined herself in. The smell of varying colours reaching my nostrils brought the dreaded memories alive.

I cannot forget the day Gurudev Lespakamanya graced our kingdom and our home with his divine-filled presence. The people, the entire way, stood silently with their eyes popped out, raising their hands in folded "Namaste" while being transfixed at the aura of Gurudev. His walk was so powerful and enchanting that not only the human but also the animals were encapsulated under his radiated aura— his straightened spine, long steps, forward-facing, totally uncaring towards the spotlight of his presence. With his one hand carrying the energy-filled water and the other carrying the *Rudraksha beads*, Gurudev walked towards the darkroom where my mother had confined herself. While on his way, a helpless cow with a swollen stomach caught his attention. He immediately stopped, went to the cow, rubbed the stomach, placed his right-hand thumb over the forehead. He then proceeded towards my mother.

My grandfather was all fearful and confused, oblivious to how my mother would react or if she would see him at all. All his apprehensions vanished into thin air, when he saw that the door was already open. As if she was waiting for Gurudev's arrival. Even I was stunned to even remotely believe that the doors were opened. My mother never opens the door, let it be for grandfather or me or anyone. *What was that? A divine agency facilitating or some celestial communication beyond our common comprehension?* Gurudev Lespakamanya advanced to the door, and called "Chitrangada, approach me, dear."

My grandfather received yet another jolt at the mysterious happenings. Never did he mention the name of my mother to Gurudev.

My mother, in a weak step, steadily came up to Gurudev and fell on his feet while sobbing uncontrollably. Gurudev tenderly placed his hand on my mother's and said, "Cry your heart out, dear. Cry your heart out. Om Namah Shivaya."

Gurudev sprinkled some water over my mother, gently smiled, and said, "Your pain is an emotion, Chitrangada. That emotion is inflicted on you by society, not from within you. Because within you, there is only perpetual energy. The energy of God alone. Invoke that. Your passion is to portray pictures. Your deepest emotion is pain. Now, emulate the emotion of pain blended with various other emotions into your passion. You will realize the supreme God. The supreme God is not in stones or objects or even in prayers. He is a spirited conscience everywhere. Once all the dust and anomalies around you are removed with the dose of awareness, you will see his celestial form. You have the almighty blessings, daughter."

He then turned towards me and looked into my eyes to say, "You have a destiny to fulfil. A lady of half-human will approach you, and realise then that your destiny has begun. History will conceal you into the smallest patches of words. Yet, the ones who know you can transcend their life just by knowing you. Two years from now, come to me and I will teach you everything of life and also nothing of life."

Even now, I couldn't make out what kind of destiny I must fulfil that Gurudev was revealing. Only time will tell. But, if Gurudev's encounter had not happened, if Gurudev's light of sagacity hadn't rubbed on our ignorance. My mother's edification might not have occurred. Her compelling eyes showering with wisdom wouldn't have propelled. I wouldn't be watching the fluorescent Chitrangada that I am presently witnessing— full of life and effulgent vitality blooming under her radiant spirit.

The days spent subjected to malicious slandering by a heedless society acted in our best interest. My mother and I were forged day in day out into impregnable unyielding spirits, like a sharp weapon wielded from burning and blazing day in and day out.

Post that day, the incurable cow started getting healthier, with the subsiding swollen stomach. My grandfather had become an ardent follower visiting Gurudev to meditate under his presence. Gradually, he began to lose interest in the administrations of the kingdom and Acharya managed the daily affairs with the active help of my mother.

CHAPTER 22

Somewhere in the Dvaita forests, 3147 BC

Carrying the *Pashupatastra*, together with the Gandiva (A powerful bow forged with one hundred and eight strings), Arjuna began his journey to the abode of Pandavas, where they were spending their twelfth year in exile. Arjuna, enroute, had come across many hermits and ascetics with whom he had the chance to spend much of the time meditating in their blessed presence, discussing life and God. Arjuna wondered *how the ascetics could meditate keeping their bare body in the deadly cold waves that would surely freeze one's heart. It's hard to imagine. Maybe they balance their frequency of breath in such a way so as to keep the body warm from inside or release heat from various body organs through the breathing techniques.*

Passing through a narrow passage onto the arid land, with not a living soul or a tree sapling in it. Arjuna finally reached the forest territory, at the southern foot of river Saraswathi, located south of Kamyaka forest in a time period of nine months. The place was bundled with an abundance of sugarcane which is only peculiar to the mainland of *Dvaita* forest.

The first one to run into him was Bheem, who was busy taming a wild elephant. Arjuna eventually heaved a sigh of relief after watching Bheem. He had not changed

149

much except for new extra muscles forming on his shoulders and stout legs. Arjuna waited, witnessing his brother's immaculate strength from a distance, adopting every possible way to bring the elephant under his control. *Oh! The meeting could wait*, Arjuna thought, marvelling at the sight of his brother bringing the mighty elephant under his control.

The fight of dominion lasted a bit longer than expected. Nevertheless, the build of the elephant could not be ignored. The loud trumpets of the beastly sized elephant frightened the birds of various species into escaping to the safest place. But the tenacious Bheem was not just a person, but a formidable force to reckon with. When the elephant finally surrendered, Bheem ascended the wild elephant and started to march away in the opposite direction, away from where Arjuna was standing.

Bheem suddenly stopped the elephant when he got hold of a few running whispers in the air, "Wait, brother. Wait!" echoed in the forest. He discerned the voice belonged to none other than Arjuna as he started a full arrayed search with his eyes filled with excited curiosity, sitting on the top of the elephant right until he captured a glimpse of Arjuna, smiling at him, with his Gandiva and Pashupatastra glued to the back.

With a big welcoming smile playing on both of their faces, Bheem hurrayed the wild animal to move towards Arjuna.

Bheem smilingly yelled, "Brother, I can barely see your eyes and teeth."

"Why is that?" asked Arjuna

"Because you are entirely covered with hair, and I suppose you need a quick haircut." exclaiming that both grinned softly at each other, Bheem gave some hard punches at the top of an elephant head, signalling the animal to bend, capture and fetch Arjuna to be seated behind Bheem. Comprehending the indication given by Bheem, the elephant obliged, gently bending on its knees, placing the trunk on the ground. Arjuna tamed the head portion for a brief moment and ascended with his right foot by placing it on the tip of the trunk. The wild beast gently lifted Arjuna and moved him behind Bheem.

Once seated, Arjuna enquired, "How did you manage to communicate with this elephant so quickly?"

"Ha-ha! Some secrets are better left to assumptions." Bheem chuckled and continued, "Brother, you have lost a lot of weight. I can see your bones. Don't worry, we will have you in perfect shape within a few weeks. And I believe you pleased Sadashiva with your austerity and acquired the Pashupatastra?"

"Yes, brother. I was graced with Sadashiva's warmth and presence. At some point, I even thought of renouncing everything behind and just moving with him, completely surrendered to his energy and engrossed in meditating on him." Arjuna continued, "he was just pure incorporeal."

"Hm! I even tried to sit for meditation many times in the past, but my mind wandered to lots of food, or sleep or working out some of my muscles. So, I realized

I am not in for it." saying that Bheem laughed out loud, followed by Arjuna.

"Brother. Please tell me, how is everyone? Especially Hidimbi and our dear Ghatu. I cannot tell you for what reason, but I remembered a lot about Ghatu during my period of austerity. His authenticity and dedication in what he does. The awakening pleasure he has acquired at a tender age by indulging in meditation. He is someone who is highly capable of provoking the both the stupid and ignorant to choose the path of God and salvation." Arjuna sighed.

"Yes. That's precisely the reason we decided not to involve Ghatu in the war that is about to unleash in a few months from now. So, Hidimbi and I are of the opinion that we should keep Ghatu away from the deceiving world. But for that to happen, we were compelled to take a hard stance, even if it's hard to digest. So, Hidimbi and Ghatu will continue their life without me in the forests of Kamyaka, which we thought would be in the best interests for Ghatu." Bheem said with a deep inhale.

"I have to agree with you on this. The kind of man Ghatotkacha is evolving to be— a devout, disciplined, and a great person with immensely gifted magical powers. The world will try every possible dirty trick to eliminate such a gifted person if he comes to light." Arjuna said

"Hm! You are absolutely right, brother. Krishna and Nakula opined that the war, if it ever happened, will be the bloodiest till date, the Bharatkanda ever witnessed. I even suggested not involving Abhimanyu with the war, for he is an adolescent." Bheem said, squeezing his eyebrows.

"What was the response from the others?"

"Well, to be specific. Everyone was muted except Nakula, who was in agreement with my opinion. I was of the conjecture that everyone's muted expressions were because of how exceedingly brilliant Abhimanyu is growing as a warrior and their reluctance to have such a ferocious warrior restricted to closed quarters. Not a soul wishes not to have him on their side. He can be a decisive factor. Krishna presumes that Abhimanyu, with active and substantial backup, will single-handedly wipe out the entire enemies to dust or make them retreat in six days. That significant effect Abhimanyu has and will have on the morale of the army that he is fighting for." retorted Bheem.

"I am unsure as to whether I should be extremely proud of my Abhimanyu for receiving the accolades from the greatest of warriors, or should I be worried for his life?" paused Arjuna, engrossed in deep thought.

CHAPTER 23

The grand jubilation—

After the departure of Gurudev, my mother opened her doors to the morning light and started to translate her deep hidden emotions and multitude of fears into emotive paintings, unconcerned and cold to society's unreasonable comments. She was free, absolutely free, one with nature, and had finally transcended into a new way of life.

My mother gave a slight jolt to my shoulders, noticing that I was lost in distant thought while offering prayers. I smiled at her and said, "Nothing, Ma."

"Aitreya introduced me to Manvi. He is so full of jubilance. And Manvi has a gentle heart. I believe she will protect him with all her heart." saying that mother turned to face the court priest chanting the Vedic hymns.

After the prayers were over, mother turned towards Rasikri and informed, "Daughter, take good care of all the guests that have come for the feast. Don't leave any guest, let it be a soldier, a brahmin or shudra, or a starving street animal. Make sure all are well fed without any qualms. Bless you, my dear," as she went on to greet Acharya, who was approaching from the front doorway.

I accompanied Rasikri to the kitchen and came across Aitreya, Manvi and Suprasena and their glorious unstoppable devouring of various food items. It was neither a shock to me nor to Rasikri considering Suprasena's unending love for food.

I sarcastically shouted at Aitreya, "Aitreya, how many times do I have to remind you not to indulge in Suprasena's company else you will fail to see your feet by standing straight roughly in three years from today."

Suprasena stood from his seated position, still carrying a *payasam* (or milk pudding) in his hand, and screamed, "I could see my feet very clearly" as he eyeballed me.

"*Chacha* (uncle), by bending one's back, even the elephant can see its whole feet." Aitreya commented.

Rasikri burst into laughter and then I. Aitreya, and Suprasena followed amidst the non-stop barks of Manvi. Even the *chief supkar* (the head of the kitchen) was not able to control the smile.

The kitchen was a site to marvel. My grandfather personally supervised the building which contained a hugely built area spreading over 350 dandas * 500 dandas (one danda equalling five feet). Total three Chief Supkars were appointed to supervise each task—

Cultivation of required crops needed for varying seasons.

Preservation of the food for a longer period using different methods of drying and fermentation techniques.

Distribution of food as per the required demand.

Twenty-four *Upakaraks* (Associates) would be reporting to one chief Supkar, where they will be assigned distinct duties. In turn, the *supremo-supkar* will continuously monitor the duties of *chief-supkar*. The above post was warily chosen with the assistance of the council of ministers as my grandfather felt that healthy nourishment of the body plays a pivotal role in one's life. Few instances of natural calamities in the past that lasted for a year and half had subsequently forced acute shortage of availability of essential food to the citizens killing many, leading to the situation mandating administration to take cognizance of the seriousness involved. The availability of better storage facilities was made a top priority for the kingdom. The food department headed by *supremo-supkar* made every possible effort and succeeded in accommodating the food to the starving citizens. All that was made possible due to the genius storage of surplus food items over a large period of time.

The supremo-supkar would directly report to the council of ministers headed by the king, appraising them on the detailed balances of receipts and payments, the requirement of finances, and the available stock of food— *ready for use and future use*. I was surprised to learn that two-thirds of the funds for the food department come from the citizens voluntarily. I realized how important the department is for the people.

The entrance to the kitchen is flanked by two hugely built elephant sculptures with raised trunks paving the way for the magnificent Iron Gate, embedded with innumerable depictions of Devas and Asuras savouring various food items. Right in the kitchen, the grandiose would further unveil. Entire walls were built with pure white marbles. The bristles of sun rays falling on the white marbles could be witnessed reflecting in the vast mirror placed on the opposite wall. The walls of the kitchen were constructed in a semi-circular manner, with the mirror placed in the common diagonal. On the diagonal wall it was, connecting the two ends of the curved marble which was made up using formidable rock each with a size of brick which was *four feet * six feet* and the thickness was *three feet*, making it impossible to penetrate.

The reflections on the mirror were used to measure the time required to prepare the food. The towering mirror was embodied with several parallel lines running from left to right numbered in an ascending order. Those lines would act as a reference point to prepare food in large quantities as per the proposed requirement. So, the morning food would be prepared with the sun rays hitting the second parallel line and would be completed before the sunray hits the fifth parallel line.

Three-fourths of the kitchen space was allocated specifically to preserve the food, placed near a square-shaped window for ventilation. Here, those specialized and experienced in preservation techniques would be employed to properly take care in ensuring that no errors were committed from their end.

The cooking area was always busy with twenty to twenty-four members attending to it— *some chopping vegetables, some cooking, and some cleaning the site promptly.* The smoke and toxic gases emitted would be routed to outside using a large vertical chimney erected right adjacent to the cooking area.

As today was the day to celebrate the valour and bravery of fellow soldiers, *Adi Atulya,* our *supremo-supkar,* a tall, medium-built man, with weak and droopy shoulders, swollen neck and a wood sized heavy moustache. With skimmed cheeks and large circular gold earrings swinging to and fro. Gold ornaments hanging under his neck embedded with glittering shiny diamond stones, head dressed with a golden coloured cloth. Adi Atulya in thorough consultation with the council of ministers decided *Mamsodana* (meat biryani) as the main course of the feast followed by curd rice, ghee rice, *Payasa* (milk pudding), *takra* (buttermilk), etc. The common ingredients used for rice items are ghee, petals of various aromatic flowers, and leaves of different plants.

Everyone was enjoying the flavour of the meal. Large chuckles echoing the hall, flying murmurs in fragmented pieces, everyone calling for the item of their liking to be served, filled the air all around. Beholding at the content and delighted sight, my mother sighed in exuberance, exchanged pleasantries, thanked Rasikri, and silently resumed to her private chambers.

When the moon was bright and round, with the nightingale song growing louder and more evident, it was time to call it a day. Everyone was pleased and satisfied, ending the friendly conversations in good spirit. They blessed the kingdom, paid obeisance to my mother and thanked Rasikri and me for the arrangements that were made as they proceeded to their ambient homes, to the longing embrace of their wives and to cuddling love of their adorable children.

I played with Aitreya for a while, gagged a few satirical giggles, and we ended up laughing out loud in the garden. After that, Aitreya, Rasikri, and I escorted Manvi to her new hut adjacent to our stay, with a thick rope tied to her leg. I could understand from the darkness of her eyes how much Manvi misses Radhasaki. But, with God's grace, she in no time had accepted us as her family and our home as her new abode.

Bidding goodnight to Aitreya, as he dozed off to a deep sleep, Rasikri and I proceeded to our bedchamber. *O', I miss the feel of my personal space.* Gently closing my eyes, I touched the mirror in a swirling motion, brushed the wooden bed slowly, and breathed the small Tulasi tree seated in the corner. My senses were never too pleased with the luxurious and exotic places, but the touch and feel of my personal room was beyond describable. After marvelling for a spell under the flowing stream of memories of my chambers, I breathed bliss and glanced at Rasikri, who was busy making adjustments to the already perfect bed. I chuckled and thought *it's always the same with her. No matter how bold and fearless she is to the outside world, once she sets foot in the bedchambers, she can't stop her mind and hands from making minor adjustments for her never-ending satisfaction.*

"Fates of various people and the biggest battles will be decided during the time that you take in adjusting our private room. Now, please get back." I exclaimed teasingly.

"Just a few more moments, Babru." pleaded Rasikri apologetically, still glued to her phobia of the disoriented setting of the room.

Finally, she arrived in my embrace. She threw a few nostalgic expressions with a teasing smile playing on her tender lips and quickly adjusted herself onto my chest. She grabbed my left arm while twirling my chest hair with her left hand. I tenderly held her in my arms, caressing her hair and softly kissing her left cheek before moving closer to her.

As we submerged into the universal play of making love. Time dissipated with each passing ether, thoughts were carelessly left abandoned by mind and our minds became submissive to the reverberating body and the stirring soul. The overjoyed beatitude lasted for a heavenly time.

Post the ethereal confluence of two empty and craving souls, Rasikri held and squeezed me tight, her head turned to the other side as she started shedding tears inconsolably. I gently turned her head to my facing and enquired about her anguish. Yet, she was inconsolable. I got up from the bed, offered her a pint of water and urged her to take deep breaths. I gave her time to recuperate, and then enquired about what had suddenly transpired into her mind that shook her off balance breaking completely into tears.

She raised her eyebrows at me sobbing as she looked into my eyes, and muttered in broken sobs, "It ha...s been sev....en years since our ma.....rriage. But, my repea...ted incompetence in giving birth to a child of your bloo...d bloodline is pricking me."

"Stop Rasikri. Not again. Please stop!" I voiced disapprovingly while offering her a mug of water.

"No, Babru. Please. I am devastated. Some nights are spe....nt without clos....ing my eyes. The guilt is consuming my soul bit by bit. My consultation with *Griha-vaidyachari* (family medical caretaker) and timely usage of the prescribed *Aushad* (plant medicines) has bore no results. And I am beginning to think that I am infertile." uttered Rasikri hopelessly

"We have a soulful and vibrant Aitreya. What else could you ask for? I fail to understand your meaningless thirst for conceiving another child. If we are blessed with a child, well and good. If not, why create such uneasiness? Just wait and see. Aitreya will reach great heights. One day, we will be called the parents of Aitreya, instead of Aitreya being called our son." Hm! cherishing the promising imagination, I smiled pleasantly at Rasikri.

"But. He is not your...,,....." Rasikri was stopped midway with a gentle finger pursing her lips to pause the gloomy thoughts encircling in her spider web of thoughts.

"Not again, Rasikri. I have already told you that Aitreya is my very existence. The first picture that flashed into my mind during the battle was that of Aitreya, you, and my mother. You, of all the people, drove my motivation to live. The very thought of protecting you gives me immense strength and pushes to fight harder and smarter. So, for God's sake, please don't traumatize yourself with an unreasonable burden of guilt. Your irrational thoughts will infect the ones you love in no time and will spoil the entire sphere of peace." I gently explained, wiping the tears off her squeezed face due to over sobbing.

"Hm...Ok..." Inhaling deeply, Rasikri continued, "There is one thing I need to tell," Saying that, Rasikri got up, moved to one of the large wooden wardrobes to fetch a blackish cotton cloth, and handed it over to me "Here, have it."

I adjusted the piece of cloth she had given me as I observed some obscure letters written on the cloth. I could make out the word "S O R R Y". From the handwriting, I assumed someone of amateur age or some illiterate had written it before handing it over to her.

She continued, "After you marched to the war, Gyanvitarna paid a visit to me." gaping into my expressions, she paused, letting the information sink into my senses.

Perplexed at the mention of his visit and startled at the slamming of the name "Gyanvitarna" in my ears. *So, how many years has it been? Six or seven year's maybe, since the mention of his name. His figure, truncated body form with a square head on the top and lengthy legs dragging his body, suddenly popped up inside my head. I cannot forgo from my mind the prided walk he emulated and the eyes with hard-angled eyebrows.*

"So. What was his prerogative for paying you a visit in my absence? Did he intend any harm to you or Aitreya?" I enquired with a strained heart, blood scorching with furiousness running in my veins. My fists tightening in a hush of enrage, breath becoming motionless and fast-paced. "Please, tell... Rasikri." I asked again, this time in a louder tone thumping my fists hard onto the nearby wooden table.

"Calm down. Babru. Calm down." In a desperate attempt to cool down my nerves, she continued, "Gyanvitarna was pleading to both of us to forgive him and has requested to pass on some of his personnel materials used in sculpting to Aitreya." she gasped and continued, "He fell on his knees, begged inconsolably to forgive him, in an open display, while I was on my way home." gently stroking my hair and kissing my forehead Rasikri said, "Please calm down." grabbing my hands and placing them on her heart, "From the looks of it. He meant no harm. Now, let's rest. I presume both of us are exceptionally tired." she teasingly commented, evoking a quick jerk of a smile to my face.

"Now, hurry yourself to your gentle dreams. I will have a few moments to myself in the garden. I need fresh air." kissing her goodnight and carrying a jug of fresh water. I quickly dressed and walked to the garden. The garden had a wide variety of flowers and trees belonging to different families, accompanying me in my solitary time.

The whistling wind was dazzling my senses with its mild strokes and wheezing resonance. I lost myself taking delight under the sparkling stars as if they were signalling to each other and communicating with me in some strange language. Sombre moon, as always looked confused and bright, was aloof and far away from the flashing stars. Chuckling to myself, imagining and making out the probable communication between the objects of the sky. The aroma of the flowers, all diverse yet mixed up, bruising my nose hither and thither, produced a sublime aroma while pleasing my senses abound.

Amidst the heavenly affair with elements of nature, I could not get rid of black cotton cloth out of my subconscious self. It kept on flashing and re-flashing and hitting my consciousness. *Gyanvitarna........ I warned him to never even remotely hope to come near Rasikri or Aitreya. Seven years. It has been seven bloody years. And he showed up. His shamelessness was further incriminating, exposing his veils of stupidity. I loathe his life. I simply loath his disgusting life. When was it? When was it that our lives were turned upside down, like a hung caricature? Ha. It all started with prudent Goklevitarna and with his nerve-ending* obsession with Vedas. Goklevitarna! It all started with Goklevitarna rushing to pay a visit to my mother, citing the urgency of the matter.

CHAPTER 24

Karna Parva, 17th day of Kurukshetra war, 3145 BC

The third commander-in-chief of Kuru kingdom, *Vasusena* was bestowed with the immense responsibility of leading the enormous army against the Pandavas. Though not royal by birth, though not a prince of extensive lands, Vasusena was a warrior of ingenuity that *Suyodhana*, the heir to the entire Kauravan Empire, had ever come across in his life. More than his exceptional skills, Vasusena was flawless in character, authentic in spirit, and the most trustworthy confidant to Suyodhana (Cousin Brother of Yudhishthira). One time, when the kings of royal lineage had denied Vasusena from participation during a weaponry competition merely because he was born to a charioteer. When Vasusena was alone defending his skills alone and pleading to be included in the competition, not a single soul came to his rescue.

And right then, a man with glistening gold armour and crown, the gold rings on his fingers shimmering with the sunlight, the profound eyes bordered with thickened eyebrows, Suyodhana rose from the lion-handled glossy throne, lifting the pearl-imbued mace onto the rugged muscular shoulders and moved to the centre of arena where Vasusena was stranded alone being abused. Suyodhana placed his hand on weakened Vasusena, instilling courage into him and moved to face the authorities. Gently caressing his bow-shaped large moustache, Suyodhana stood tall and bold. He dismissed the sheer madness of every royal dignitaries present, rebuked the impoverished mind-set of every person who were in the process of branding a skilled worthful person based on birth and denying the very person the deserving accolades. Suyodhana lamented the pure deadly infection that was seeping into the annals of society taking the monstrous form of discrimination based on royalty, power, caste and creed.

Standing tall as a mountain with his chest held high, Suyodhana announced, "If ruling a meagre land acts as a qualifier to participate in the competition, then I am offering my *Mahajanapada* (a larger state) — *Anga*, to Vasusena for his ruling. I believe his capability and far-sightedness in ruling the land prosperously, exceeds anyone who is sitting in the podium discussing the birth of the prodigious warrior. I pity the ignorance of the disgusting individuals present. I fear that the land of the great Kuru dynasty falling in the hands of petty mind-sets who in the name of scriptures openly embrace discrimination based on birth. Even if needed, I will fight with all my might to not let this land fall into the hands of conservative and conventional fools. Henceforth, Vasusena will be called to, as crowned king of Anga, the brother and dear comrade to Suyodhana."

No one dared to oppose Suyodhana, including *Grandsire Bheesma* and *Guru Dronacharya*. Such was the charisma of Suyodhana. That moment was a divine revelation to Vasusena, that very brief, Vasusena surrendered the likes of his life to the cause of Suyodhana.

Watching Arjuna and Krishna from a distance, Vasusena felt both retribution and guilt thumping on his chest. Vasusena longed for the arrival of this day, the day when his arrow will be emptied of all the blood lust after it has ebbed away the life of Arjuna. To Vasusena, the raging vengeance was not to prove to the world that he had dominated Arjuna. But, the dominion was essential for the world to have knowledge of the righteous Arjuna, who never rightly stood for the righteousness that he so openly claimed of. *The sting of envy in the eyes of Arjuna unable to witness a forest dweller going by the name of Ekalavya showcasing far greater bowman ship compelling the poor innocent warrior eventually to cut-off his finger, or for that matter, his absolute inaction when his wife Draupadi was being disrobed in public, or his muted expression and bitterness beholding my archery skills and openly supporting the theory of disgusting discrimination of status derived from birth,* Vasusena mused.

At the same time, Vasusena's guilt was ripping his soul into pieces. The guilt of betraying Suyodhana swept through the conscience of Vasusena when he had forgoed the lives of Pandavas when he had the chance to slay them. Vasusena was always caught in the spider web of choice between his unflinching friendship with Suyodhana and the vow he had made to *Kunti* for her preplanned begging request. Kunti's treacherous plot on the night of the fifteenth day of battle, by confronting Vasusena and offering a revelation of her relationship to him as his birth mother startled Vasusena.

Vasusena stood astounded as he listened to what she had revealed to him that night before the coronation of commander-in-chief, explaining with a proper timeline of events. There was no iota of doubt that her sequence of evidence would in any way be wronged. *Hm! There she is. Standing pretentious. False tears pouring. The vile mother who was ashamed to call me her son. Abandoning me into the river, fearing the wrath of society. The same mother who stood there witnessing and marvelling when everyone was ridiculing my birth during the competition. This is the same mother who didn't have the courage to inform the Pandavas that I am their eldest brother. If she had, the war would not have happened. Yudhishthira, my younger brother, would abdicate the claim to the throne in favour of me. When the throne is in my hands, I will most happily endow it in favour of Suyodhana, or even Suyodhana might not accept it, considering me as the heir. The deaths numbering in lakhs would have been easily avoided had this ego-centric lady announced to the world that I am her son, the eldest of the Pandavas. But she didn't. And now, why now? At this odd time of hours, she wanted to disclose her identity? What could possibly be her vicious intentions?* Vasusena pondered for a while and enquired, "Lady, now is not a good time to fend relationships amidst the pearls of destruction. You have had the chance many times in the past to disclose your relationship whatsoever you are claiming to have with me. But, you chose not to say it. I completely

169

understand that you might have had your own reasons. But, I must tell you that I will, and I can never consider you as my mother. Only *Shrimathi Radhadevi* is my divine mother and my only mother. She never cared for the opinions and remarks of society while raising or nurturing me, nor did she discriminate against me anytime with her own children. I believe those are the traits of being a mother which I suppose you have none of. But I must admit to you, you opened my eyes into realising how great and virtuous my mother Radhadevi is. That much credit you are entitled to receive. So, lady, your arrival in requesting my audience is not a coincidence. That too, warily choosing the night before I will be announced as commander-in-chief. So, please state the business of your presence."

Kunti sobbingly said, "My so...n, nev..er a mom.ent has passed with..out a thou...ght of yo...u and your well be..ing. Even if my bo.dy resides in clos..ed quart..ers with my five s..ons, my hear..t always aches for y..ou."

"Please state your business, lady. I don't have much time for your millennium melodrama." Vasusena clamoured in a loud voice.

"Ok then. All I need from you is a word of honour." Kunti asked without looking into the eyes of Vasusena

"Ha! There you are. I anticipated your devious intentions the moment you showed up, proving your motherhood. Perfectly knowing, I will not turn down the request. Since, you decided to come to pay a visit." Vasusena continued abominably, "You have my word. Ask whatever you desire, including my head. I will happily offer the same."

"No, son. No. Don't use such harsh words. I never wish any of my children to die. So, I pray to you to please pardon the lives of your five brothers."

After a few moments of thought, Vasusena said, "You have my word. I will pardon every life of your son except Arjuna. I assure you, even in the future, we will be called to as Pandavas."

That vow compelled him to pardon the lives of mighty Bheema, Yudhistara, Nakula, and Sahadeva. Vasusena had the best chance to slay them and please his friend, Suyodhana.

Now, when Vasusena was gazed at by Arjuna and a cunningly smiling Krishna in the battlefield of Kurukshetra, he felt all the vicious accumulated rage ready to burst into the open like a volcanic eruption. When Vasusena watched the vengeance-driven Arjuna standing erect with his chest held high, he couldn't help himself from brooding over young Abhimanyu, resembling substantially the physical features of Arjuna. The dreaded circumstances even compelled him to wrongfully take part in the immoral and disgraceful act of assassination of a lone warrior such as Abhimanyu. Even the righteous Dronacharya couldn't keep himself from this sinful act. Everyone was equally convinced that the only way to eliminate the stormy threat of Abhimanyu was by employing unlawful means. Abhimanyu's single-handed fierceness had decimated eighty thousand soldiers to dust and every powerful person succumbed to defeat. Abhimanyu's valour did not spare the lives of *Brihadbala, Lakshmana— the son of Suyodhana,* and the seven foster brothers of Vasusena. He even managed to defeat in one-on-one battles with *Dronacharya, Kripa, Ashwathama, Suyodhana, Dushasana and Vrikshasana* in one-on-one combat. If Abhimanyu was left to be haywire in the battleground for one more prahar, he would have brought the entire Kauravas clan to its knees with a shameful defeat. That was the immeasurable strength and potential that Abhimanyu had possessed. So, everyone was convinced that the only way to subjugate Abhimanyu was through employing unlawful methods. *That was the moment Vasusena realized that they had lost the war.*

CHAPTER 25

The prodigious virtuoso—

It was mid-noon; the blazing Sun was right above our heads. My mother was watering the freshly planted saplings. I was there. I was there conversing with my mother. She elucidated about different types of saplings and the time it had taken for it to grow into a full-grown plant. I had wondered how some trees could live more than three hundred years. Suddenly, a female caretaker rushed towards my mother and informed her about Goklevitarna waiting outside the mansion, citing it was an urgent matter.

Mother passed the watering jar to me and hurried to the waiting chamber where Goklevitarna was waiting.

Goklevitarna exchanged warm greetings with my mother as she ordered the caretaker to bring some coconut water. She seated herself opposite Goklevitarna and asked, "Please grace me, minister. What do I owe you for this sudden surprise visit?"

Goklevitarna replied, sipping a gulp of coconut water, "My Queen! A few days before, as you might remember, you were looking for the person who was sculpting in the forests."

"Yes. Indeed" replied mother as she grew curious.

Goklevitarna exclaimed in a proud and thrilled tone "Well. It was not my son as you had anticipated. He never deviated from his duty to the Vedas, hymns and……. "

He was cut short by my mother in between.

"Do you happen to know by any chance the person who is responsible for those sculptures?"

"Yes. It was my son's friend—that dusty, spoiled, uncouth, and poor person. *Bhatukesh.*" said Goklevitarna in an annoying manner.

"By any chance, do you know where he lives, minister?"

"In the suburbs, Queen Chitrangada. Right at the backyard of our market."

"Sincere thanks to you, minister. You may take your leave now. Apologies for taking up your valuable time." She stood up, and with a gentle smile, folded her hands in a 'Namaste' by bidding him good day. Without a moment's delay, she instructed the search party of soldiers to fetch Bhatukesh from the suburbs to the kingdom.

The people of the suburb were petrified to notice the presence of kingdom soldiers at their place. Never had they witnessed such a large congregation of soldiers in the past. Every time the visit used to consist of a small entourage. But, this time it was different. They were even more surprised, shocked, and confused when they saw that the soldiers had halted near Bhatukesh's small hut which was made up of wood and the roof enveloped with firm turf of grass.

In no time, the rumours started to spread like a raging fire. *It might be that Bhatukesh is a criminal. Have the soldiers come to detain Bhatukesh with heavy chains glued to his legs? Was he being taken to get beheaded?* Petty murmurs grew louder and louder, and the chit-chats were only getting stronger and more profound. Suddenly, the noise collapsed into complete silence and awe. As astonishment began to seep into the psyche of people.

The sight of various gifts in the form of food and copper plates were being offered to the family of Bhatukesh. The music being played was giving utmost honour to Bhatukesh's arrival. This information startled and shook the onlookers.

Bhatukesh was puzzled and perplexed when they requested him to take a seat on the top of the elephant, which he had never done in his life. His family was entirely new to the limelight and attention they were getting. Bhatukesh thought *that either the kingdom had gone mad or had confused him for another person, which will soon be sorted out,* he mumbled within himself taking a nervous gulp. But Bhatukesh was overjoyed at seeing his parent's content and was delighted to receive the honours from the king himself. He had never seen his parents so happy. It made them feel like heaven. But Bhatukesh's brother was unsettled and doubtful, thinking about what deeds his hopeless and ineffective brother had performed that attracted the recognition from the kingdom.

When the entourage began its journey to the palace, carrying Bhatukesh in a grandiose way, leading from the front, on an elephant. Jubilant and nervous, thrilled and disturbed, Bhatukesh saw Gyanvitarna waving at him from a distance.

Bhatukesh signalled Gyanvitarna to come near him. When Gyanvitarna reached his ear length he perceived the perplexed look on Bhatukesh's face. The latter informed Bhatukesh to meet him before proceeding to the Queen's guest chambers.

When the privileged entourage reached the kingdom, the trumpets filled the air with their heart-pounding sound and music. Bhatukesh got down from the elephant and began searching for Gyanvitarna. Suddenly, he got a punch from behind and realized it was Gyanvitarna.

"We don't have much time. Just pay attention to what I am about to say." Gyanvitarna muttered cautiously.

"Gyanvi. I am shitting my pants. You hear me. I am shitting my pants. Only the devil knows how much I am confused and worried for my life. I don't know what has transpired into the ministers, a haunting ghost? Get me out of here, Gyanvi. Somehow. Every moment spent in the limelight is killing me from inside. Just do something." Bhatukesh pleaded.

"Ok. Here is the truth. They think that you are the architect of the rock sculptures." expelling that piece of information, Gyanvitarna waited for the effect to sink in.

"What the hell? That was you. What madness has gotten into them to think of me as a sculpt...ure." Bhatukesh chuckled with a breath of relief, "Thank you, Gyanvi. I will tell the Queen that it was Gyanvitarna and that they are mistaken."

"Absolutely not. Bhatu, here is the catch. They are not mistaken. I repeat, they are not mistaken."

"Then?"

"It was my father who informed the queen that you, the Bhatukesh, made the sculptures."

"But, did you not tell him that it was your doing, Gyanvi? I mean, it was your love and soul and inspirational art." Bhatukesh chided, completely taken aback by the information.

"I tried to, Bhatu. I tried. When I was about to tell him, when I was trying to tell him, my father started abusing and belittling the art that I adored with all my heart and passion." In a disheartening tone, Gyanvitarna continued further, "When he pressured me to give him the name, unable to take the coercion anymore, I blurted out a lie. I lied that it was you, that it was my friend, Bhatukesh, who had sculpted the deserted, lifeless rocks into vibrating souls."

Bhatukesh, seeing the teary-eyed Gyanvitarna, consoled him by holding his hands in his, "Don't be disheartened, Gyanvi. Of all the friends I know how celestial and sublime you become when you indulge yourself in sculpting. It's like witnessing the living God in action. Please, tell me now what should I be doing? How can I be of help to you? I am ready to do anything for you, Gyanvi." hugging Gyanvitarna with a smile and proud chuckle playing on both of their faces for being friends.

"Thank you, Bhatu. Our deep-knotted friendship is the reason that I had to take your name for my name. Thank you with all my heart." wiping the face in a swift, Gyanvitarna continued, "Listen, from what I have learned from one of my trusted sources close to the Queen, that she is a prodigious painter herself. So, when they are to receive you with grandeur. Offering you praises, gifts, holding discussions and arranging lunch or dinner with the highest dignitaries itself." discovering the excitement rubbed on Bhatukesh's face, Gyanvitarna gave a gentle push on his chest and continued, "Don't get carried away. Here is the tricky part. Queen Chitrangada might ascertain your credibility as an artist." elevated excitement turned into a pale expression. But, Gyanvitarna continued, "Ha-ha! Now, your devilish disorder of multiple personalities has come to light." with a bit of teasing sarcasm and jest, Gyanvitarna laughed.

"Stop it, Gyanvi. Now, please continue. I don't have much time. See the soldiers over there, they are watching me as if I am their mistress." both mildly laughed at the comment made by Bhatukesh.

"Alright. Alright. I have handwritten every minute detail about the sculpting in running notes— The type of stone required, suitable stones for sculpting, the pressure dynamics used, the time it consumes to hammer different layers of stone, the kind of art you select, the final touch of sculpting, etc. Memorize the technical part of the note quickly and you have got less time. So, try to memorize as much as you can and deliver it with confidence so as not to raise any suspicion about your duplicity." saying that, Gyanvitarna asked, "Anything you want to say?"

"Nothing. If I get caught and killed. Just look after my parents." replied Bhatukesh nervously.

"Nothing of that sort will happen to you. I will take your leave then. Stay focused and confident." assuring him that, Gyanvitarna was about to leave

"One more thing, Gyanvi"

"Be quick"

"Don't you feel betrayed or forsaken?"

"Why should I be, Bhatu? You must be mad."

"Because someone else, some unworthy brute, such as me, is enjoying all the luxurious rewards at your artful expenses and your worthy genius. Don't you have any remorse for not getting well-deserved recognition for your deeds in art?" Bhatukesh enquired with a compassionate tone.

With a slight chuckle, turning his eyes inward, Gyanvitarna said, "Bhatu, only the luxuries, gifts and grants associated with my art, with my sculpture, are not being conferred to me. Isn't it? Now, please tell me. Can you or the ministers or the God himself snatch away the art, or my soul emulating the art? The answer is plain no. Before this moment, I have had the gripping fear that my father would get a sniff of my sculpting and rusticate me from the roots of my family.

Now, that element of fear has disappeared. Imagine with no fear attached, with no burden of parental conditioning, just imagine the kind of aesthetic and high-spirited art I can produce on the rocks. Meanwhile, you can enjoy the rewards." gently patting on Bhatukesh's cheeks, with a soft smile, Gyanvitarna continues, "I am proud to say, you are the reason for the deliverance of my freedom." With that being said, Gyanvitarna disappeared into the crowd.

CHAPTER 26

The Crown of Grieving Hastinapur—

Even with the war won, even at the helm of Hastinapur, Pandavas troubled minds had reached a new zenith of turbulent misery. Surrounded by countless deaths of kins, family, near and dear ones, the thought always and every time prickled the conscience of Pandavas. *What if the war did not occur in the first place? What if their mother Kunti divulged the identity of Vasusena to them as their elder brother?* These unsettling questions troubled Pandavas to no extent.

When Krishna informed Arjuna, the person he joyously killed and celebrated was none other than his elder brother. Arjuna's body went numb with shame and utter chaos. Aggrieved and furious, Arjuna, inflamed with intense disgust, admonished his mother for her foolish act of withholding the truth.

On the other hand, knowing the truth about Vasusena, It dawned upon Yudhishthira that the reasons their lives were spared by Vasusena when he had the best chance to execute them during the battle was due the promise he made to their mother. Yudhishthira's anguish had hit a new low. After learning the dreaded truth about his elder brother, he felt the futility of winning or participating in the war. *Those warm eyes, when he pardoned my life with his tiny smile. O' Rudra!*

Condemn me to the deep trenches of hell, for I was unable to understand my brother's love. For we had committed fratricide, a condemnable sin. All his life, he endured the pain so oppressive. Even we had our part in outrageously humiliating him in public for his low birth. Even then, my impudent mother's heart remained hard and cold. Blessed was Suyodhana, for he had the love, warmth and had spent much time with brother Vasusena. With that thought wheeling in his mind, Yudhishthira went to Kunti and said, "For you are responsible for the deaths of innocent and poor souls, for you have withholden a small truth. If the truth were in the open and known to the world, only peace and love would have flourished all over the kingdom. So, I, the son of Pandu, curse you and the entire womanhood, that you will never be able to withhold even the smallest of information henceforth." Saying that, Yudhishthira fell on his knees, and tears of melancholy rolled down his cheeks. Hands glued to the eyes, Yudhishthira let out a long noise of wail, venting out all the accumulated dirt, guilt and disgrace with one large wailing shout as he remembered the words of Suyodhana at the time of his death when he inquired curiously to Suyodhana, "Why he was smiling? The kingdom was lost, and the brothers and their children were dead. Why was he still smiling moments before his death?" Yudhishthira had enquired.

Suyodhana replied, "Yudhishthira, I pity your life as a king of Hastinapur. What would you rule? A kingdom with half its citizens lost to death? What and with whom would you savour and relish the accomplishments of the aftermath of the war, Yudhishthira? With your beautiful sons and powerful kings dead? What possibly is there for you to take pleasure in?" chuckling out loud, Suyodhana continued, "I had lost the desire to rule from the day my companion, Vasusena, lost his battle to the death. Now, all I am waiting for is this soul to reach the abode of hell or heaven or to the worlds beyond human comprehension, to wherever Vasusena resides, that is where my soul finds solace."

Noticing the grief-stricken Yudhishthira stretching on for months, Dhritarashtra, Gurudev Vyas, and Arjuna begin to worry about Emperor Yudhishthira's state of mind and the welfare of the kingdom. Every possible explanation with riddled spiritual stories had been tried to motivate and bring back Yudhishthira to his senses but to no avail. Yudhishthira was unable to resume normalcy, still brooding over the deaths of his dear kith and kin.

Troubled Arjuna was growing anxious as he watched the condition of his brother deteriorating. So, he requested Krishna for a solution to resume the ruling into normalcy and end this traumatic behaviour of Yudhishthira that was affecting the welfare of the kingdom— the farm output, the increasing trade deficit with neighbouring princely states, and collection of taxes.

Krishna acceded to the request and convinced Yudhishthira to undertake *Ashwamedha Yajna* for one full year to declare supremacy and control over the entire kingdoms of northern Bharatkanda. The Yajna usually involved continuous philosophical debates dwelling on the subjects of goodness, dharma, life, death, austerity, *Shunya* (nothingness). All compiled in the texts of *Anugita Parva*. Once the Yajna was initiated with Anugita Parva, a sacrificial horse would be decorated in accordance with the scriptures after a recital of all the Vedic hymns in praise of various Gods of Thunder, War, Fire, Wind, Water and Space.

Krishna and Yudhishthira identified Arjuna and *Vrishaketu*, the surviving son of Vasusena, to lead the *Ashwamedha Yajna* with one Akshauhini of the Army— 21870 elephants, 65610 horses, and 109350 infantry excluding 21870 chariots. They were strictly told to follow the horse wherever it went and claim hegemony over the kingdom when the horse would pass unopposed. When the horse was captured by any belligerent king, then a war was waged against the state for denying the king's sovereignty.

The horse was left off-guard from the city of Hastinapur on the third day at the first light. It moved on its own wherever it pleased, and just before the departure of the army, Yudhishthira moved to Vrishaketu and said, "Your simplicity and mannerism resemble your father. I made a promise to your father that you will be looked after with all dignity like a dear son to us. So, please be cautious and always be in the footsteps of your uncle, Arjuna." saying that, Yudhishthira hugged and sobbed with all his heart out while remembering his brother, Vasusena.

CHAPTER 27

The demonic transition—

Bhatukesh was the happiest person on the planet. He was getting special attention in the neighbourhood and society. The floating luxuries at his doorsteps, along with the joyful jubilation of his parents were beyond describable for Bhatukesh. On the other hand, Gyanvitarna, the most contented person in the universe, was marvellously reflecting the gentle lives on rocks getting fascinated and exuberantly lively with each passing day. Every moment was perfectly crafted except for the weaving toxic thoughts peddling in the mind of Goklevitarna.

When everything was working perfectly for everyone, the unsettledness and agitation started groping Goklevitarna. Because he was a primal minister. He was duty-bound to witness and spectate every single event with no exception. From the time he was assigned with the duty to administer careful displacement of rock sculptors from the forest to the kingdom, for the instalment at the various corridors or entrances of the kingdom according to the theme of the natural setting of the place.

With the active help of Suprasena, my mother was primarily engaged in the placement of each specific sculpture at a suitable place. Whenever there was a new arresting sculpture, immediately there was so much celebration and adoration for Bhatukesh and his godly sightedness.

Witnessing this, every time with his own eyes, Goklevitarna cursed within himself for why there was no admiration for his prodigious son, Gyanvitarna. But the fact that a boy from the poor suburbs, Bhatukesh getting all the fame and attention, irked and tormented Goklevitarna to no bounds. On many occasions, Goklevitarna wondered why his son was not a sculptor?

The growing envy towards Bhatukesh transmuted into vileful abhorrence little by little, day by day, getting ready for eruption any moment. The peace-filled atmosphere in Gyanvitarna's home was many times spoiled by the unwarranted frustration of Goklevitarna. No one dared to neither question nor oppose such an inhospitable behaviour because they believed the raging fumes would evaporate with passing time. But little did they know, the fumes thus discharged were accumulating in stages in the subconscious psyche of Goklevitarna.

Once, when Gyanvitarna had finished an awe-inspiring rock sculpture depicting *a herd of elephants quenching the thirst of exhausted warriors.* The soul of the sculpture impressed my mother so tremendously that she arranged a feast for the entire kingdom in the name of Bhatukesh. Even Bhatukesh could not believe his eyes when he marvelled at the humongous sculpture full of life and emotion and couldn't help but feel endless guilt for stripping all the credit for the divine-filled sculpture that he is not rightly entitled to. But the feeling of immense contentment in the eyes of his dear friend, Gyanvitarna satisfied Bhatukesh a bit.

That fateful night, following that ominous day onwards, the accumulated raging fumes erupted into a dreaded storm engulfing every component of peace in Goklevitarna's sweet abode.

That eventful night, when Gyanvitarna returned home only to find crushed clay plates spread all over the floor. His mother was seated in a corner wailing and sobbing with dreadful fear looming over them and engulfing her from inside. Her swollen cheeks were towering on her face. That trembling sight of the frightened mother shook Gyanvitarna to numbness and voicelessness. That was a ghastly sight, which no son wishes to witness in his dear loving mother. The devoted mother, who knew only to give love and whose happiness lies in the children growing healthy and steady. Gyanvitarna was forced into witnessing the horrendous happening with his own eyes. He could have asked her, "What happened?" he could have offered her water and consolation. But the sight numbed his voice and spirit, and he stood there watching her with a heavy accelerated heart. He stood there, watching her. He paid no heed to her warnings. Her repeated warnings to Gyanvitarna to leave the place for the day. Her repeated requests to her son to run away for the night did not reach the conscious self of Gyanvitarna.

A little while later, Goklevitarna emerged furious in a never seen avatar before, hurling abuse after abuse at Gyanvitarna, thrashing him with his leg or with any objects that were within his reach. Gyanvitarna was shocked beyond belief to see his own disdainful father pounding thrash after thrash with continuous abuses. "You shameless imbecile, you witless moron, you proved me a failure, you have brought shame and indignity to the family."

Listening to this, Gyanvitarna was unable to comprehend the offense he committed. He inquired in a low tone about what had happened that infuriated him so much. The query further infuriated his father so much that his mother was victimized. Goklevitarna did not stop there. "That worthless greasy, bastard scum, Bhatukesh. That dusty foot was getting all the accolades and appreciation for that unmerited and valueless sculpting that only the deprived and lower sections of the society indulge in."

This comment made Gyanvitarna realize the reason behind the rampage, that his father was unfolding. The veil of goodness that he covers himself with was finally removed. His true nature was out in the open. A pure insensitive zealot is all he proved to be, Gyanvitarna realised. He thought of telling his father that he was the sculptor and Bhatukesh was just a bogus creation created to escape from his wrath and hatredness. But he decided against it, beholding his beaten mother and his father's insolence. The flying abuses and thrashings, "You worthless shit. Good-for-nothing insignificant product that your mother produced." As he went on thrashing his mother. "How many hopes I had for you to carry the proud lineage of our family. And such a despicable person you proved yourself to be, Gyanvitarnaaa... spineless son of great Goklevitarna. That you cannot even win a Vedic competition against a girl, a poor girl, a peasant, and a low life girl." As Goklevitarna spitted on Gyanvitarna.

Wiping the saliva off his cheeks with his bare hand, touching mother's feet in blessings. He fixed his gaze on his father, Gyanvitarna grew closer and stood up to face his father as he decided to reveal his identity as an artist and uttered in a hushed voice, "I am the sculptor, Goklevitarna! The glorious slave to the kingdom. Fearing your wrath, I renunciated all the appreciation and accolades that were due to me. For all I care for is art alone, not the riches that come with it, not the accolades that follow it. And I am never returning home to your bonded enslavement." thumping his chest twice and thrice, Gyanvitarna left home in a fit of rage unmindful of his mother's wailings requesting him to stop. Not a word dropped from Goklevitarna's mouth as he stood there shocked watching his son disappear.

Gyanvitarna went to Bhatukesh's home the following night and called him out, citing urgency. Watching Gyanvitarna at his doorsteps, Bhatukesh rushed outside, checked Gyanvitarna thoroughly for any injuries and said, "Gyanvi, your father is frantically searching for you everywhere. In fact he visited me in the morning and requested the whereabouts of you. I felt pity for him when he started sobbing and had requested forgiveness from me. I didn't understand him. Thank god, you are safe and sound. Let's go, Gyanvi to your home."

"No, just follow me," Gyanvitarna replied. And they both went far away along with one another friend of theirs, *Giriraj*, who had arranged food and other requisites on the way.

The place in the forest was a secluded one, located deep in the cave with a small opening at the top. The only light source of light was the glistening moon at night. Without a bother for the uncertain danger of predatory animals, the chirping beetles of the forest, the howls of wolves, they sat upon the ground. Giriraj placed the freshly cooked meat with ghee rice on a bamboo leaf and passed it to Gyanvitarna. Giriraj and Bhatukesh exchanged frightening glances with each other as they comprehended from the expressions of Gyanvitarna that something terrible had transpired. Else Gyanvitarna would be the one to initiate the talk and jest and make everyone around him comfortable and smile. But something had gone wrong, something very unpleasant, they perceived. Bhatukesh requested Gyanvitarna to have something to eat. A while later, Gyanvitarna started to eat, his face still malicious and enraged.

After some time, Gyanvitarna started to talk and vented out his frustration by narrating the whole incident about Goklevitarna's cruelty. This was probably the first time Bhatukesh noticed Gyanvitarna was addressing his father by his name. Giriraj, contemplating the dejection of Gyanvitarna, suggested bringing local made indigenous liquor. Bhatukesh and Gyanvitarna initially showed reluctance as this was their first time but later succumbed to temptation. Liquor has reached and slowly started to take effect. After a prahar (three hours) of intoxication, all the time, all Gyanvitarna voiced in a grossly intoxicated state denounced Goklevitarna, empathizing with his mother, belittling and denigrating Rasikri for his continuous failures.

With each passing day, the liquor poured in doubled, intoxication reached a high, providing them a momentary solace. The annoyance of Gyanvitarna all together deviated from his father into slandering Rasikri and her continuous winning spree unabated. Gradually, under the influence of liquor, positive affirmations from Bhatukesh and Giriraj and stemming strong hatredness toward his father completely blinded Gyanvitarna into believing that Rasikri was the prime reason for his miserable state.

One fine evening, when the birds were returning to their nest following sunset with the emerging dark clouds. The moving and growing gloomy clouds erupted in lightning thunders, signalling a heavy rainfall. Families were in a rush to clear all the spices and dried clothes in a bid not to expose them to rain.

The heavily intoxicated Gyanvitarna and his friends gazed at the desperate Rasikri bringing in all the sheep under one roof from a distance. Giriraj's eyes feasted on mildly drenched Rasikri as he made salacious remarks on her body. Bhatukesh joined the chorus, but

Gyanvitarna was unmoved, fixing his intense stare at Rasikri's every moment. Bhatukesh discerned the lustful stare of Gyanvitarna. He was immensely shocked but pleaded with Gyanvitarna and Giriraj to move away from the place. However, Gyanvitarna paid no heed.

Gyanvitarna ordered Giriraj to survey the surroundings. He did as asked and reported that not a soul was to be seen in the falling radius due to the heavy occurring rainfall. Families locked themselves in their respective huts, Rasikri's parents were not at home. She was all alone.

Terror and panic jolted Bhatukesh when he realized the lustful intentions of Gyanvitarna and Giriraj. Cursing them for what they were about to do, throwing light on how warm-hearted and amiable Rasikri is. He warned them about the repercussions and subsequent execution that would be given by the kingdom. However, these consequences didn't even evoke a reply or alarm from them. Gyanvitarna and Giriraj, with their ceased sense of reasoning, dampened minds, their blood induced with an unquenching thirst for liquor were driven by the inexhaustible craving for unsurmountable eroticism.

Bhatukesh ran away with his heavy body lumping forward, gasping for breath, heavily soaked in the impounding rain. Reaching his hut, he watched the female figure that he adored and respected— his mother who offered him food lovingly. *The picture of Rasikri politely receiving him during the celebrations, friendly chatter they had, the small banter of laughs,* everything flashed before his senses. He shivered and shivered at the horrific thought of the violation of a woman's body and spent the night with the heavy throbbing of heart and the continuous flapping of eyelashes, and without the blinking of sleep.

Gyanvitarna, continuously flooded his body with pint after pint of the liquor, followed by Giriraj. They approached Rasikri's home and requested food for the night. Upon recognizing Gyanvitarna from the Vedic fair, she welcomed them in and fed them. However, upon realizing the insobriety of the guests with the emanating liquor smell, she was quick to request them to leave as it was getting late for night. But her repeated requests were responded to unfavourably.

CHAPTER 28

Arjuna appointed Vrishaketu as the chief of battle formations. Every time Arjuna held his hands or beheld the sight of Vrishaketu, he couldn't help but get haunted by the chilling memory of him firing his arrows at his helpless brother Vasusena who was off the chariot upheaving the struck wheel. Arjuna said, "Vrishaketu, whenever a king captivates the sacrificial horse, use the battle formations that your father had taught you. We will be victorious, I am sure of that."

Arjuna, Vrishaketu, and the army started marching towards the northeast following the directions the horse was wandering in. They were met with no resistance and hostility in a few countries. But the descendants of *Trigartas* posed a great danger. They subsequently captured the horse, and challenged Arjuna to combat.

The *Trigartas* had a long history of holding vengeance and carrying intense hatred towards the *Pandavas* since the time of their forefathers. Carrying that animosity of vengeance inside their heads, the king of Trigartas, *Suryavarman* attacked Arjuna and the army with full prowess only to realize the attack was so trivial and petty before the powerful Arjuna. Soon, the brother of Suryavarman, *Ketuvarman* attacked Arjuna with full might, and Arjuna mocking his stupidity, executed

Ketuvarman after an intense exchange of arrows on the second day.

Upon the defeat of Suryavarman and execution of Ketuvarman, the younger brother, *Dhritavarman* showered a continuous barrage of arrows at Arjuna. Arjuna was startled and impressed at the lightning speed with which Dhritavarman was handling the bow and releasing the arrow. Teased for a while with Dhritavarman until an arrow pierced his golden armour, enraging Arjuna fiercely, compelling him to release his celestial weapons decimating the Trigartan army, ultimately forcing them into surrendering to the emperor's sole sovereignty.

After the annexation of *Trigarta*, Arjuna and the army followed the horse, moving in the eastern direction. They successfully managed to annex many princely states and smaller kingdoms without any resistance En route. But, soon the horse entered the territory of *Pragjyotishpura*— the land of mighty elephants. Arjuna knew that they would be rugged defiance from the *Narakasuras*. Late King *Bhagadatta* of Pragjyotishpura fought the Kurukshetra war in support of Kauravas.

On the twelfth day of the Kurukshetra battle, when Bheem was hurling strong punches with his mace at Bhagadatta's deadly elephant *Supratika*. Bhagadatta, mocked at the sheer childishness of Bheem for even thinking of attacking the mammoth Supratika. He ridiculed Bheem and moved to fight with Arjuna with whom he thought he equalled in courage. He invoked the use of *Vaishnavastra* on Arjuna. But Krishna, using his magical power, thwarted the pounding Astra (weapon) and reduced it into a garland of flowers. In that split of time, Arjuna brought down powerful Bhagadatta by firing a potential arrow aimed at his chest. Since then, the son of Bhagadatta, *Vajradatta*, had been waiting for a chance of retribution for his father's death. When Vajradatta was informed of the sacrificial horse belonging to Pandavas, his elation knew no bounds as he himself was planning a strategic attack on Hastinapur to avenge the death of his father, and ironically fate had brought Arjuna straight into the clutches of his land.

Vrishaketu was growing impatient from waiting on the outskirts of Pragjyotishpura and told Arjuna, "Uncle, why are you not giving the order to move in? From the looks of it, we could assume no one has captured the horse."

Arjuna replied, "Vrishaketu, I killed his father. If my calculations are anything to go by. Vajradatta is waiting like a wounded lion for us to step inside his kingdom and brutally attack and reduce us to a bare minimum. He is dangerously powerful in his own home. So we will wait!"

Two days passed for Vajradatta to make the first move. And then, he let the wild elephants loose onto Arjuna and the army. The elephants numbering in hundreds were running wild with ear-splitting noise of the trumpets. The settled dust and the rocks were hovering in the air with the wild steps of the elephants. Arjuna discerned that Narakasuras had instigated the elephants by using spices into the elephant's nose and eyes.

Without getting intimidated by the incoming menace, Arjuna jolted Vrishaketu's shoulder, who was stunned to numbness, gaping at the mammoth-sized mammals with the tree-sized trunks and instructed him to form the battle formation targeting at deflection of the elephants.

Vrishaketu instructed the army of soldiers to arrange themselves in the shape of a 'Sword' battle formation. Using the large pointed spears as the main defence encapsulated the archers in the centre of the battle formation aiming at the elephant's eyes.

Arjuna stood proud witnessing the brilliance Vrishaketu was displaying in the war with the leadership skills and battle formations. No doubt the ingenuity of brother Vasusena was passed down to him, he thought. Arjuna knew the size of the mammal never matters when the target and preciseness of aim were well in alignment.

Arjuna, observing the approaching elephant at him, drew a sharp and long arrow made of iron metal and aimed at the spot situated right between the elephant's eyes targeting a small gland hanging under its brain that holds the entire life of a living being. This knowledge he acquired from study of anatomy of animals from Guru Dronacharya where he had practically evidenced the position of the gland in a dead elephant by dissecting the upper layers of the head. A brief moment later, muffling his vibrating bow into unerring stillness, he let the arrow loose and set-out the target of the small gland. *The size of the elephant did not matter to Arjuna neither did its dangerously hideous trunks, nor its earth shattering thumps. His focus was beyond the fathomable. His target was way beyond the elephant's eyes. For he saw neither its body, nor the skin. A gland, a gland that hangs at the base of every brain of mammal, is what he picturised his target at.*

In a snap of time, Arjuna had showered one hundred and ninety four arrows at the advancing elephants. Thirty-two elephants fell to the ground, instantly emanating a large thudding sound with wailing trumpets of the befell elephants.

Witnessing the swiftness and accuracy Arjuna employed with the bow, Vajradatta was appalled at the skills of Arjuna and petrified to the bones at the thought of facing him in the battleground. *No man or any Asura ever managed to bring down the perilous elephants of Pragjyotishpura in a matter of few moments just like Arjuna had,* Vajradatta thought.

Gazing at Arjuna's brilliance with the bow, Vajradatta wondered, *there was absolutely no hint of fear visible on his aging face. His mind and spirit are devoid of the ambiguities around him during the war. His bow, arrow, hands, fingers, eyes, body posture, and stillness of the mind looked as if amalgamated into one single form.*

Vajradatta realized the futile exercise of fighting Arjuna and surrendered to the supremacy of Yudhishthira. He was fairly convinced and glad with the choice he had exercised, for he didn't want to put the citizen's lives at risk and jeopardize the magnificent infrastructure his father had built so dearly for the sake of vengeance. It would take years to bring everything in order.

Arjuna, happy with the wise choice Vajradatta made, expressed gratitude and regret for the execution of Bhagadatta and explained the inevitability of consequences of war which Vajradatta graciously accepted.

After bidding farewell to Vajradatta, Arjuna followed the horse that was moving further south. Upon reaching the path leading to large mountains, Arjuna faintly remembered the blurring images of the natural landscapes, the cooing of birds, the whistling of the wind, and the calm beatings of the water bodies. *Have I visited this place in the past? Not in the last two decades. Never. I might have crossed the path in my youth during one of many of my youthful traverses. I cannot explicitly recall,* wondered Arjuna to himself, beholding the sight.

When one of the traveling experts briefed Arjuna that the country the horse had set foot in was *Manipura* and was prosperous for trading with countries beyond the borders. Arjuna was intrigued and startled to learn that a woman actively rules the kingdom without any qualms and disagreements from the society. *The people and the country might be one of the most advanced and cultured land, emphasizing on gender equality, equal opportunity, near absence of discrimination, and most importantly, non-segregation of society that is rampant in Hastinapur,* thought Arjuna. Quite impressed with the ruling, Arjuna was beginning to grow more curious and anxious to meet them. He felt the need to emulate the culture of Manipura into Hastinapur— the ideas of importance of women, absence of segregation of society, the scope of foreign trade. Arjuna believed the city he was about to conquer will greatly help him in modernising Hastinapur that is rotten with caste, closed economy and over dependence on tax collections of princely states.

CHAPTER 29

The manifested savagery—

Throwing an inconspicuous signal at Giriraj, Gyanvitarna insidiously smiled at Rasikri. A sudden quick jolt was blown at Rasikri's back of the head by Giriraj with the wooden mug placed on the ground. The ache bolted her into the landscape of calamity, and Rasikri hammered onto the ground with a heavy thud. With blood rolling from the nose and crack on the skull, oblivious to the tribulations she was about to endure, tormented tears begin to roll down her cheek, compelling her to plead for her life.

Gyanvitarna relishing the excruciating agony being inflicted on helpless Rasikri— her repeated pleas, the transpiring helplessness, every sort of distress gave immense amusement to Gyanvitarna's senses. He felt himself to be a triumphant God, taking pleasure in the long overhauling wails and taking pleasure in the dreaded moments of her agitated cries. He felt undefeatable and infinite glory, when he violated the physical body of Rasikri over and over again. *Many images sparkled in Gyanvitarna's mind— his childhood spent trying to win appreciation from his father, which he never achieved. His self-immolation of his passions to please his father by trying to learn Vedas he never liked, which too was never achieved. His soulful seeking of self-esteem by doing what he does best, the art of sculpting that too was ruined.*

201

His mother, his loving mother that he never wished to grieve, that too was spoiled with the self-centred barbarian, his father. His moaning growing louder and louder and more painful with each reflection of the past events was suddenly thwarted with the interjection of Giriraj's strong clamour, "Gyanvi. Stop it. Stop it. You can kill her. Now let's move out of this place before someone catches us."

His breathing steadied slowly as the intoxication faded substantially, Gyanvitarna moved away from the place with a cold-blooded face overflowing with a sense of fulfilment and accomplishment. *Finally, he felt he had avenged his father in the thickness of Rasikri's floating blood, his long-held bitterness in the deepest tunnels of his soul was finally unleashed amidst the brutal violation of a helpless adolescent.*

But, there was one element that Gyanvi missed— he unleashed a deadly demonic force inside of me.

Suprasena and I wondered what might have befallen Rasikri for two days. She was completely shunned to silence, restricting herself into four corners of her home, and her vague denials became repetitive whenever she was asked to come out for horse-riding or some other activity.

The very next day, while I was practicing sword fencing with my master, I saw Bhatukesh nervously striding to and fro with endless knuckle-cracking.

After finishing my practice, I was taken aback for a moment realizing Bhatukesh was on my feet, crying out loud, and asking for forgiveness. I gently raised him and waited for him to calm down. I then asked what was troubling him? *I could see the horror dripping down his face in sweat, mumbling and struggling to catch the words.* I again requested him to calm himself down and enquired the second time about what had happened?

My mind was permeated with voidness and my nerves were running at a rapid pace. My limbs went numb and utter chaos flushed in my eyes as my cheeks went red, listening to Bhatukesh's whole narration of the horrific exploitation of Rasikri's innocence and her helpless soul plundered with lust-filled fanaticism of Gyanvitarna and Giriraj.

I whispered in a sharp tone, "Why did you run away that day, and why did you not feel like cautioning me the same day itself?"

"I am sorry, Prince. Please forgive me. I didn't do any harm." Bhatukesh whimpered while crying out loud.

Hissing angrily and breathing heavily, "How much have we valued you for the art that was not done by you. If my mother finds out that you are nothing but a bogus person, her spirit will be broken, and she will trust no more of any person." taking out the sword from my right curve, I demanded by shouting, "where will I find him now?"

"In a cave. In a cave!"

"Precise. Be precise." I howled.

"Deep into the jungle, cut by a small waterfall!"

In a swift motion, I slashed my sword, slicing his right-hand off from his witless body in one swing. Blood bashed in my face. I gently rubbed the blood-off my face and whispered, "Consider this my offering to you—your life. I am sparing your life. Your inaction led to the chopping of your hand, and you cannot claim innocence, for you did nothing. In fact, you did nothing even though you had the choice of doing the right thing. You had the privilege of direct access to my mother or me and had the chance to save an innocent girl."

Terror filled the onlookers, and my sword master stood there, watching me in awe. Unmoved, straight into my eyes from a distance. I took out the chiselled knife and attached it to my right torso. I held the budging head of Bhatukesh steadily, pulled out his tongue, cut it out as I threw it at a plant full of lemons and said, "This is for you to stay silent for the rest of your life. If you even try to pass on the truth of abuse of Rasikri using any other means, either by writing or facial expressions, I will feed your body to the rats."

I was trembling and fluttering uncontrollably, *O' Sadashiva! the ruminating thoughts of young, joyful, and cheeky Rasikri chasing the sheep, her gags at our cracking jokes, her boldness, her sensational intellect of Upanishads and Vedas, her growing up into a beautiful woman,* everything, every far-fetched memory of her started to crumble before my eyes like falling broken stars of the wretched night. I ascended the horse, unaware of the yelling's of my mother from behind, gave a *Hurrah!* To the brawny horse to lead us into the cave, to the bastard sons.

I could visualize Rasikri struggling against the animalic weight pounding on her flesh, pleading with them with large wails. O' Dear Lord! The beholder of every momentous happening! How could you witness and allow such barbarism? From the stretch of the first ray to the vanishing evening light, I searched for the wretched scoundrels. They were nowhere to be found. I was beginning to get desperate for reprisal. Still searching for Gyanvitarna and Giriraj in the corners and open lands of the forest. There was no sight of the crooked animals. Then, in that moment, in that silent chirp of the insects, I perceived the murmurs and the wandering steps of the humans, with emerging flames in the forest.

There they are! Without a ping of guilt on their faces, widely arrayed laughs echoed in the forest, the liquor was flowing through them. They were marching back to the city.

When they stepped into the open on their way home, they watched me approaching them, and shouted in a belligerent tone, "Who the hell are you?"

My breath was becoming harder and heavier watching their faces with unbalanced bodies. Words twisted in an intoxicated medium, and Giriraj said, "This man near me is the lord....lor.d of seven worlds. Do you hear me? Lord of seven worlds." and they erupted in a deceitful laugh, and Giriraj continued, "Do you know that? You miserable human being. This man has conqueeee...;"

The sentence did escape Giriraj's mouth but was left half-finished. The blood spurted out from the top of his neck and filled the ground. The head landed at a distance of two feet from the slain body. I retrieved the blood-filled clean sword back to my scabbard, wiping it clean from dead Giriraj's clothes.

I waited for Gyanvitarna to come to his senses. I waited for him to realize my identity, break his intoxication, and comprehend the reality. Gyanvitarna, unable to understand the jolt to his drunkenness, incapable of making out the circumstances that he was in, questioned in a large howl keeping both his hands to his head, "What the hell is happening and whyyyyyyyy?"

I calmly replied, "Decontaminating the area from lustful worms."

Gyanvitarna's long wails were for no one to be heard, as there was no single soul to be seen for a large distance. Finally, he came to his senses, broke down on the ground and cried out loud, "Sorry....sorry......I would do everything in my capacity— raise her and compensate her, for her entire life. In fact, I will marry her." Sobbing and wailing, he further continued in a broken voice, "Please, I beg you, I beg you to spare my life."

I scoffed at his arrogance and stupidity. *Marry her as if she will reach heaven after receiving his pity. Marry her. Ugh!* I stood there, listened to his bizarre pleadings as I took out my small curved knife off my right torso and said,

"Bhatukesh, narrated to me your entire filthy life. I reckon you adore your art with your life."

With a crack in his voice, Gyanvitarna whimpered, "Yes! With my life."

I gently held his right hand, caressed his palm and in a quick flash, hacked his ring finger and thumb of both the hands in a swift wink of his eye. Blood splurted upon his swollen face and on the surrounding ground. He yelled for life. The pain took a toll on his emotions, and he yelled and yelled with increasing sneezing and the flow of tears.

I had listened to more apologies on that single day than any other day. I gazed into his eyes, cuddled my knife, gently passed on a small cloth to ease the leakage of blood and I said, "Gyanvitarna, you intend to marry the person you violated. Your very violation itself was her disapproval. Isn't it? So, you are confined to treating every woman as an object and only as an object of desire at your disposal" watching his horror-filled eyes and his trembling gut-wrenching body, I said, "This is my punishment to you. If I kill you, you can only experience the pain for a few moments. So, I am sparing your life. I believe you will not dare to even go near the sight of Rasikri in future. I will leave your body as disgusting as a worthless animal, helpless and unable to sculpt with remaining fingers, and incapable of speech with your tongue." blurting that, I cut his tongue and squeezed it inside his mouth to swallow. I filled his mouth with whatever left out liquor that was lying near to Giriraj's body.

When the first ray of light hit the day, the dreaded horror of slaughtering of Giriraj, amputation of Bhatukesh, and the chopping of Gyanvitarna reached out and sent shivers across the city. Everyone's head turned in my direction. My mother was appalled by my rage of carnage and violence. There was a high-level inquiry into the incident. Having witnessed the aghast of me slashing Bhatukesh's arm, my sword master informed the inquiry team of the same. When the team mentioned my name in the killing of Giriraj and their gruesome incident, the frightened Bhatukesh and Gyanvitarna shuddered their heads into saying "NO" thereby clearing my name from the murder of Giriraj. But, the kingdom held me responsible for the hacking of Bhatukesh's hand. So, I was punished with banishment from the kingdom, for two long years."

My companion, Suprasena was initially angry and disappointed with my actions. Upon knowing the reasons behind my vengefulness, and realizing what meted out to poor Rasikri. He was burning with rage and admonished me for why I had left them alive. We made sure that not a soul will get a sniff of what transpired with Rasikri.

Right before my banishment from the kingdom, I took my mother's blessing, evidently she was disappointed and furious with me, and I went on to pay a visit to Rasikri. Waiting at her doorsteps, Suprasena was already fussing about how bad an idea it was to meet Rasikri at this juncture. Finally, she opened the door with the face of a defeated and crushed soul, large bruises evident over her cheeks. Yet the elegance did not escape her. She was all about doing fine and coping up well. It was noticeable how bad in shape she was—fragile, shallow-eyed with her sluggish hands resting on the door. The moment she said, "Thank you for coming to see me." with a broken and feeble smile half running on her lips, I lost my strength and vigour.

That moment, looking into her dim eyes, fathoming her unwillingness to leave my sight for two long years, a long-buried mystical emotion escaped my soul which resulted in me uttering, "I would love to marry you, Rasikri."

Soon, absolute silence flooded the atmosphere. Suprasena was gaping at me in astonishment as if a thunderbolt had hit him. *My gust of love towards Rasikri was never out of sympathy or compassion. I realized the seed of my love for her started from the day we were pupils of Gurudev Lespakamanya. Every memory popped up. Every mischievous thing I did in a bid to impress her or witness her smile. And, today, the realization dawned upon my longing soul.*

Without a blink of an eye, she said, "Yes."

Suprasena narrated the whole incident to my mother Chitrangada. Involving Gyanvitarna and his friend's connection in the brazen violation of Rasikri. Breaking down with swarming eyes, mother wished to see Rasikri immediately. Suprasena requested my mother, the matter be kept a secret to avoid denigration of Rasikri. Then he informed her of the marriage and how I had proposed to Rasikri. Mother was elated for this union of Rasikri and me. Immediately, she had sent a man on watch duty to inform grandfather and Gurudev Lespakamanya.

When mother arrived at Rasikri's home to greet her and have a word with her parents, she could not hold back her tears, witnessing the always joyful and cheerful Rasikri in a distressed and broken state. I requested my mother and elders to have the marriage in close quarters. She vehemently opposed and refuted the idea. *Maybe, her nightmare of memories in marriage to my timid father flashed in her mind that forced her into saying no. But, I wouldn't leave Rasikri as my cowering father did!*

The marriage happened in a grandiose manner with the active blessings of my grandfather, whom I see rarely as he had chosen the path to salvation, and Gurudev Lespakamanya, who I understood, knew about everything that had taken place. Gurudev Lespakamanya blessed us. He ordered Rasikri and me to go east of the kingdom to a small river and set up a hut there. We were to spend two years engrossed in household duty and meditation during the period of banishment.

After a few days of marriage, I proceeded to the east as advised by Gurudev. We set up a small hut and built the home together. We were living the life of *Nirvana* (blissful heaven). However, two months later, Rasikri was grieving gloomily near the river. When I enquired with her about the reasons, she replied that she was carrying a baby in her womb. We both understood the gravity of the matter. Both of us chose to remain silent as an escape from the wretched truth. After the marriage, we were never physically intimate. As I surmised, her bodily emotions had become aversive to external human touch, more precisely, the male touch. We never discussed it. I thought, *only time will transcend her body into a youthful budding state.* After a few days of silence, I went to Rasikri and said, "I am ready to be a father. I feel blessed and blissful that Lord Shiva has chosen me as the mentor, a guiding light, and a spiritual teacher to the child that you are having."

After musing over the past events for almost one prahar. I looked at the cotton cloth containing the inscribed letters that Gyanvitarna handed to Rasikri. I smiled at the appearing image of Aitreya shimmering with joy.

I went as noiselessly as possible to the bedroom where Aitreya was sleeping and kissed him on the forehead and placed the sculpting material near to his bed that Gyanvitarna requested Rasikri to handover to Aitreya. I gently closed the door and thought, *God bears witness to my love for Aitreya. Maybe Aitreya carries the blood of Gyanvitarna. But, he bears the soul of mine.*

FINAL CHAPTER

The surveillant party rushed to my personnel chambers to request an audience with me. They cautioned me on the imminent security risk that was approaching the kingdom. When I greeted them, I could apprehend from their anguished expressions that something very threatening was dawning upon us. Just as they started to explain about a decorated white horse and some Ashwamedha Yajna that I frivolously had no idea about. The impending repercussions of capturing the horse results in inviting the wrath of the son of Lord Indra, the supremely feared warrior of the North Bharatkanda.

Son of Indra! Are these guys serious? Wow. I thought.

At first, I was utterly confused in making a connection between the capture of the horse and the dreaded war. Astonished and baffled, I probed the men of the surveillant team to elaborate on the irrational horse ritual and its affiliation to war. One man, well versed in Vedas, came forward and expounded the theory behind the ritual, which was ultimately instituted to claim imperial sovereignty. This was very detailed in the scriptures. My eyes surged to disbelief at the insignificant horse ritual and its immoral sacrificing by the end of the year, which incensed me into thinking about what kind of world that we live in. Only God knows the plight of citizens living under such a rigorous and incongruous belief system that they have designed.

If an animal, a horse, was subjected to such senseless cruelty under the veil of scriptures, I could not even imagine the kind of limitation the women would be subjected to. Now I understand why my grandfather, on the advice of Guru Lespakamanya, insisted on comprehension of Upanishads, while stating the limitations of Vedas.

I called for the convening of the emergency meeting with the ministers chaired by my mother. The intense debate was carried out, with many displaying signs of apprehensions at the arriving threat. Some even contested our lack of preparedness and absence of befitting weaponry in facing this celestial weapon the warrior carries. Acharya Astabhargava too was at a loss of words and loss of a crafted plan to counter such a large scale of weapons. All I could notice from their countenance was fear and fear for their life. Never in the past had I witnessed such grim faces terrified at the hostile forces. This was one such exception.

I stood up, observing the chaotic environment and bashed the wooden table hard enough to rattle the flying noises into silence. When I had their attention, I spoke. I spoke with the mind of not a slave begging for life but like a man of insight. I spoke not about the damage the celestial weapons could cause but about the damages our surrender to them will cause to our belief system. I spoke not about the future but the enslavement of mind and spirit if we surrendered. "Lives! The lavish homes. The mountains. The breeze. The air. I fail to understand your vision for the future, ministers! Life, yes, we will be spared but freedom? The freedom of choice? The freedom of will and expression?

What about that? We will be forced to adapt to their insane culture, to their system of discriminated mindsets, forcing our women to mere objects of desire at their disposal. Would you of all the people present here, with God bearing as a witness to our testing time, want that to happen?" I roared at the beholders, thumping my chest hard with my closed fist.

Toughness rejuvenated and blood pumping through their veins, they repeatedly shouted, "No, no, never," banging the wooden table over and over again.

"This time, we will fight the war for the children. For children are the future and the carriers of this historic day and they need to learn to live and breathe with freedom of rationality and resist the wrongful tyrants." I bellowed with all the energy.

"For the future." Everyone clamoured.

"For the future!" everyone shouted in unison.

I then requested Acharya to formulate a plan of action in safeguarding the lives of the citizens in case of a security breach. I asked my mother to assist Acharya. I requested every minister except Durvasana and Suprasena to administer courage and remove nauseating fear before it engulfs their minds.

Even if I postured boldly at the meeting, Durvasana and Suprasena knew of my raging fear inside my skull. I couldn't help but think all the time of the power of celestial weapons. Never had we faced such a weapon nor had we acquired one such but, we only got to know about their power from the songs of bards.

"The weapons of God
Once given a Nod!

Wrecks havoc and spreads horrors
Wipes out mainland's and farmlands

Alike we dust the path
Withal the weapon bathes
With the blood and bodies and the ruins!

The weapons of God
Invoked with a chant
turns trees of green
to ruins of dark,
turns blues of sky
into the darks of clouds.

Invoked with a chant
The weapons of God
butchers and massacres
living things into dust and oblivion!"
The bards used to sing.
"So, what's the plan?" Durvasana asked.

215

"Don't know. Neither formations nor any poisonous arrows would work this time. Arrange the army under your command, Durvasana." I sluggishly said, humbly patting on his shoulders.

I asked Suprasena to capture the horse and hole it up in someplace that only he would know. I shook his hands, hugged him, and Suprasena went on his way to do his duty.

On my way out of the debate chambers, my mother hurriedly stopped me at the door and pantingly said, "Gurudev Lespakamanya was waiting for you in the hut. He has requested a few moments of your time."

I was surprised by the visit of Gurudev. As my memory goes, he never paid a visit to anyone. Everyone seeked him. *Either he is in dire need of help, or there is some sort of emergency.*

He was seated with his legs crossed in *Padmasana* and hands clasped in gyan mudra. I touched his divine feet and paid my obeisance. Followed by a few moments of silence, Gurudeva said, "I know of your angst, son. Why do you look at it as a celestial weapon of God? Why not look at it as just a weapon harnessed by a human with devoted mantras?"

"Gurudeva, my people, their homes, the lives of soldiers, everything will be wiped out in a matter of time. I don't know how to counter a weapon capable of such mass destruction. It's a bloody one-sided war." I said in a broken voice.

With a quirk of a gentle smile, Gurudeva said, "Son, remove the veils of confusion. It is clouding your

216

judgment and inner light. Once you are as calm as a river, you will perceive reality. Just remember, the war you are about to fight is the war that you were fighting since your seeding. The war is not between two powers or persons or kingdoms. The war is always between your inner spirit and the dubious mind. A moment will arrive while you are facing the enemy. A minute light will sparkle inside you, expelling all the darkness surrounding you. In that moment, you will no longer be yourself. You will no more be a human or a king or the son of Chitrangada or a citizen of Manipura. You will be just pure light— one with the universe. And you will become the universe. That moment, a power beyond your comprehension will be unleashed. You just need to utter a small word to direct that energy. The lethal energy thus generated will extinguish the enemies in a flash of time. Let me warn you, use the energy wisely. Victory to you, son."

Holding on for two prahars, Arjuna watched an army of soldiers emerging from the entryway. Now, he was sure that the country had decided not to surrender to Yudhishthira's sovereignty. Loud thudding noises were heard coming from the *Manipura* soldiers, banging their shields and weapons onto the ground, signalling that they were not easy to budge in. Arjuna ordered Vrishaketu to form the army in a defensive position.

Vrishaketu urged, "Uncle, why can't we use eagle formation and finish the battle on day one itself. From

217

the looks of it, they seem to be from the countryside using basic weapons."

"No, Vrishaketu. We cannot risk underestimating them. We will observe their strategy, planning, stability, and the durability of their attack during the first half of the battle. Then, we will decide on our next move."

One man from the left flank approached Arjuna and whispered into his ears, "Sir, the man making an appearance in the centre of the frontline with a large black dog is the Prince— the mastermind and the son to the queen."

Arjuna closely observed the tall figure of broad shoulders, stout legs, square-faced with mild beard, falling hair onto the symmetrical chest, hazel green eyes with sharp nose ending in sultry lips and thick eyebrows. Arjuna was in awe as he watched the Trident with a two-headed drum imprinted on the prince's right-forearm. *It was clearly evident, the man he was about to face, was an ardent devotee of Lord Shiva,* Arjuna thought. For a moment, the memory of Abhimanyu befell Arjuna's conscious self, beholding the physical features of the prince from a distance. The man was accompanied by a mammoth dog, passing hand gestures at the soldiers ordering them to fall in line. His calm demeanour and composure remained unperturbed. Arjuna shouted, "We don't want war. Release the horse and accept our sovereignty."

So, this is the man of celestial weapons, completely armoured from shoulders to thighs, leaving the loose hair hurling between the chest and back of the spine, holding the heavy bow onto the ground with the left hand. The bow was a marvel to witness, appearing as large as the man himself. *Hm! He must be quite a man, I must admit, for handling such a beastly large bow.* I gently closed in on Durvasana and whispered, "I thought only the horse was decorated lavishly." and we both chuckled softly.

After a few moments, I screamed, "We too don't want the war to happen. Stop barging into our homes and get back to where you have come from, and we will release the horse." After a few moments of silence, I thought

So war it is!

Durvasana, quickly comprehending my glance at him, gave orders to forty-two thousand archers to get in line to release the ineffective wooden arrows at the hostile fleet. The arrows were released swiftly in no time. As they landed, they got deflected from the enemy shields without injuring even one.

Everyone in Arjuna's army laughed their guts out loud at the fired juvenile arrows except for Arjuna. Vrishaketu, grinning widely, approached Arjuna and brokenly said, "Uncle. I cannot believe these amateurs. The grandchildren of these dabblers in the future can

proudly tell the tales that their forefathers had the chance to face the mighty Arjuna. Uncle, I believe we have wasted enough time. Please take a momentous rest. I will finish the war forcing them into complete surrender."

"Vrishaketu. Prepare the soldiers for ground attack employing eagle formation. I want every soul of those arrogant scoundrels to die and to beg for their low life." Arjuna ordered at Vrishaketu, outraged at the audacity by Manipurans.

Durvasana and I quickly comprehended that our provocation and the taunting mockery by firing ineffective arrows had incensed the leader and hurt his immeasurable pride which had prompted him to immediately change the battle position into eagle formation to launch a full-on attack on us.

I could not keep myself from admiring the accurate Eagle- formation contrived by the soldiers carrying the shields occupying the front line. The archers were in the middle of the eagle, hailing shiny steel arrows at us in a disciplined unison. Their forward march, one step at a time created a large thud of sound with their flawless coordinated steps. It was a stroke of genius achievable only with devoted practice and discipline. Every step with their resonating "huaaaah!" in synchronization had already shuddered our army flank. Even my heart was racing like a wild horse beholding their war approach.

We anticipated the fierceness and advancement of their arrows, so we brought boulders into the battlefield to deflect the hailstorm of arrows. Some managed to land from above the head, piercing our serpent-shaped shields and finding the mark of heart, lungs, arms, shoulders, and even killing instantly and grossly injuring many. Had the boulders not been placed, the casualties would have been much larger than expected.

With each proceeding step, their momentum got deranged, and the soldiers kept on faltering, significantly mutilating themselves, drawing pools of blood by stepping onto the trap we had laid for them. Their legs and bodies stuck in the sharp spears we had laid excavating large parts of the land encircling our kingdom.

Appreciation seemed too small for the commendable genius of Suprasena, who provided the idea and design of planting spears in the deep dugout lands encircling the kingdom and shielding it with a rough, thick sheet of an upper layer of shrub plantation to avoid suspicion. That phenomenal stroke had saved a lot of energy and lives. The surviving soldiers were retreating, carrying the dead and injured soldiers along with them. We didn't attack.

Just when we were in the perception that the hostile enemies were withdrawing their forces, Durvasana and I thought they had conceded defeat. I ordered the immediate soldier to pass the message to Suprasena to fetch the sacrificial horse and hand it over to the retreating forces. It was then, we saw a man of golden armour, stepping forward alone in a composed stillness, with a massive bow followed by a dozen soldiers carrying a quiver each of different metal, filled with thousands of arrows.

Our eyes gaped in astonished silence at the approaching persona emitting such aura. His serene steps were neither of surrendering nor of seeking dialogue but to proclaim his invincible prowess. For now, we understood that his self-pride was rattled with our acts of astuteness but now, he seemed as though he would shatter the entire world to retain his lost self-pride.

Witnessing the staggering eagle -formation bit by bit, fellow soldiers losing their lives to the unethical trap groomed by the pubescents enraged Arjuna to storming fumes. He fiercely instructed Vrishaketu to call the surviving soldiers back to the camp immediately. Vrishaketu had never seen his uncle so infuriated in the entire Ashwamedha Yajna. But today, the game was different. Arjuna's forces were diminished by thirty-one thousand soldiers to the concealed pit with thousands of spears in it.

While every soldier was retreating, Arjuna moved forward, keeping his spirited mind in a state of tranquillity. When he reached a certain point on the ground, he ordered his assailants to leave the quivers and head back. Arjuna studied the enemies for a while, moving from left to right, and lifted the heavily built double-curved bow *Gandiva* high into the sky with his left hand. With sun rays reflecting from the glorious body of the bow that was equipped with one hundred and eight strings. He towed the bowstring right to the shoulder using the right index and ring finger and jilted the bowstring at once, breeding into a tenacious sound of "Lions roar" echoing transiently through the hills, the sky, and into the minds of every living person in the nearby vicinity. Soldiers back in the camp blew the conch shell right unto the moment of drying the air out of their lungs, signalling to the enemies that Arjuna was ready.

I was stunned by the valiant poise he was tenaciously exhibiting. The reverberating sound of the bowstring echoed and blanked our senses to strange delusion. For a moment, we thought we had lost our hearing sense to the sharp, biting sound. Upon the silence of bowstring, conch shells filled the air with engraving resonance. In those flash of moments, the tall man was stationed with the glittering bow. The men that were carrying the quivers were heading back to their camps, placing the quivers on the ground, leaving the man all by himself. The men were screaming their lungs out, "All glory to *Swetavahana Arjuna*, the undefeated." over and over and over again.

I stopped Durvasana, who was engaging the archers to shoot arrows, and instructed him to quickly order the soldiers to take cover, forming a defence position. Durvasana shockingly said, "But, prince. He is just a one man standing with a bow." and continued, "I think we can subdue him."

Something pricked me, or some uncertainty overshadowed my senses. I could feel a menacing storm brewing over us. I didn't reply to Durvasana, keeping my eyes, my body, and my spirit glued at the sole man standing.

He raised the bow, and within a few shreds of minutes, the entire army of ours was entrapped with thousands of arrows surrounding and bordering us. Dark clouds shrouded the blazing sun above our heads. It was impossible for the rain to occur in the hot climate. But, the pouring of rain has just begun. Not a single arrow pierced our soldiers. Only God knows what his intent was and what was about to happen. Durvasana, stupefied at the happenings, raised concern, "Are we doomed?"

I thought maybe I was daydreaming. And I wished I was dreaming. A single man capable of firing thousands of arrows in a snap of time. Is it even remotely possible to herd dark clouds amidst a hot temperate day? What was that? Who was capable of such mysterious speed and accuracy? I replied to Durvasana, "I cannot tell what's happening. Just take cover." and I let Manvi loose to run for her life.

A short while later, we heard the deafening cries of the soldiers from our left plank. They were ambushed with venomous dark-skinned serpents that had infiltrated into their ranks. Soon, there were dreaded screams from every direction about the crawling cobras numbering in thousands.

Arjuna fetched the silver quivers containing the curled arrows with sharp pointed tips, mentally assessed the distance between him and the forces, and started to rain arrows in a swift artistry aimed at surrounding the entire division of soldiers. After he marked the men surrounded with the curled arrows, Arjuna released the final arrow, invoking the vitality of *Nagastra* (Snake-weapon) into it by chanting few Vedic mantras. After the *Nagastra* was released and pierced to the ground, it churned out the dark clouds. The heavy lightning with the rain followed and ignited the entire spectrum of arrows that surrounded the Manipurans into bewitching the venomous reptiles from every corner of the lands and hills and the farfetched water bodies.

The heart-breaking horror swept through the entire army. All I could witness was swirling snakes biting the arms, necks, limbs, whatever it got its hold of with its pangs. Many braved their efforts swaying the snakes but were soon swelled by the voluminous dark reptiles all over their bodies.

After half a prahar of the ominous horror, the once healthy bodies kept crumbling into the ground, throwing droplets of blood. Some were drowsily walking hitherto, while others were uncontrollably shaking. Many were paralyzed on the ground while some men's eyelids were dropped so low. In less than a prahar, I could see barely thirty thousand men standing astute, and three-fourths of our soldiers had already lost their lives to the deadly reptiles.

Durvasana broke down on his knees, wailing and wailing, beholding the near apocalypse. I couldn't see his tears as he was swamped with heavy rain, yet I can discern his angst. Never had I seen Durvasana battered so severely. I gently lifted Durvasana and requested him to safely rescue the surviving brethren back to the kingdom to be taken care of.

My heart freezed watching the dreaded dismay, my body numb with my thoughts dissipated. With the heavy gush of wind and pouring rain, the deafening lighting crushing the mountains, the image of the warrior carrying the bow then and now visible under the flash of lightning. Carrying that image of the warrior and the dreaded horror, I seated myself in *Padmasana*, clasping my little and ring finger with my thumb finger in *Prana Mudra*. With my still mind and placid spirit, I took a deep breath, taking all the appalling pain, death and the remorse into my body with one deep breath. Then, all of a sudden, *I was floating in the semblance of plenary darkness. The oval-shaped giganteum of darkness was assimilating every little thing and the whole into it, engulfing it. My pains, my horrors, my past, my relationships, my high-octane moments, were being absorbed into its black oval energy.* And I lost myself with that one breath into the ethereal of unknowns.

226

Arjuna contemplated the complete wreckage that *Nagastra* had unleashed. The brightened day had been forced into darkness inundated with gush of rain. Realizing the retreat of the surviving army back to their kingdom, he concluded that they had successfully managed to win.

He ordered Vrishaketu to prepare the diplomats to engage in dialogue with the queen of Manipura to decide on the transition of power and size of taxes they had to pay henceforth to the Emperor Yudhishthira. Just then, he observed a strange phenomenon with the prince of Manipura. He seemed to be seated in the position of Padmasana, with his eyes closed. Arjuna closely scrutinized the cruising madness manifesting into something incomprehensible. The plentiful of lethal snakes started to surround him, coiling all across him through the waters, swarming towards him. Neither the snakes were biting him nor was the man himself frightened by the deadly reptiles. But he was surprisingly unmoved from his Padmasana. Then, in the spur of the moment, he stood fearless, unmindful of the hissing snakes all over his body, and fetched a thin metallic blade nestled around his waist. The metallic silver-coloured blade was a three-layered one. And he whipped the blade in the air, slashing through the rain droplets, clearly revealing its length as good as the size of an elephant. He lashed the blade hardly onto the ground with his right hand, while his body rotated by jumping in the air. With each lash, a few dull silver-grey fireballs were churned out and were dropped into the rainwater of close vicinity.

Arjuna, baffled at what he was witnessing, further centralized his focus on the prince and his mysterious manifestation. But, the spinning of his body, the flexible arcs, and the lashing of the blade onto the ground and bulk rock structures nearby was growing intense with each passing moment. The fireballs were gaining velocity, momentum and the reach was growing closer and closer to where Arjuna was standing.

Arjuna was startled to see the large snakes decimated to smoke particles upon the impact of fireballs falling on them. *What are those emanating fireballs? What engulfing power does it carry? Never had I come across such a weapon.* Before he could understand the character of the fireball, before he could even warn his soldiers to lay low, the ambient dark-clouded sky was painted grey with the smoke of the fireballs, and the fireballs kept tumbling on the soldiers, spawning a large hole of impact at the point of contact. Even the rocks and large trees were sustained with large dug holes upon the impact of the raging fireballs. Within a quarter of a prahar time, Arjuna could determine the apparent bloodshed in his camp that led to the shrinking of his army in half.

Never had Arjuna stepped back from the war, no matter how dangerous the threat was. But the devil consummated dance form of the prince compelled Arjuna to hide behind a strong rock and witness the mass annihilation. The wild mammals of the forest were disoriented and running in all directions, crashing into the trees and the rocks and tumbling on the ground. The men En route were no exception from the cursed carnage of the fireballs.

Confused and scared, incensed and compelled, Arjuna retrieved the *Pashupatastra* that he never intended to use. A voice was telling him from inside not to use it. A voice was pleading with him to be compassionate towards humankind and the animal world. Arjuna was very well aware that once invoked, *Pashupatastra* could not be recalled. Even Lord Shiva himself cannot halt the Astra once invoked. The Astra would not stop until it completely vanquished humankind. Arjuna held the *Gandiva* and positioned the arrow horizontally at a dwelling between the eyebrows. With half-closed eyes, he invoked the *Mantra* (chanting) that Lord Shiva himself had bestowed upon him.

"*Om Namo Bhagavate mahapaasupathaya*

thulbalveeryparakramay tripanchanyanay

nanarupa......"

The mantra was left unfinished as he received a heavy jolt to the strong upper chest armour in an impulse and was tossed away a few steps back, falling to the ground, and splashing in the water on impact. For a moment, Arjuna did not understand what had transpired as he thought *where is my Gandiva that was in my grip moments before? Why am I placed on the ground and unable to raise myself?* Until he realized that his impregnable armour was cracked into two halves. A part of chest was missing the upper skin, the blood was rippling like an offended river sinking into the water changing its colour, and the excruciating pain started to monopolize his senses. Arjuna gently secured his ripped-off chest with a heavy cloth of the lower thigh portion to minimize the blood flow. Arjuna's breath slowed down as his heart started beating faster, and hallucinations overwhelmed his fragile mind. *Pictures of his childhood started to appear to his senses. Him playing, hiding under the bushes, pranking his brother Bheem. The image of adolescent Ekalavya cutting off his thumb on Dronacharya's request for traditional reciprocity of student-teacher relationship. His son, Abhimanyu's oval bubbly cheeks when he had barely started to walk.* Arjuna closed his eyes and blacked out completely motionless.

I don't know what had transpired in those surreal moments. My mother repeatedly clamoured, "Babru, stop......please stop."

I was jolted back to the veritable reality. It took a moment for me to realize that I was surrounded by palpable destruction. *Wild animals lying motionless, snakes fluttering with their half-cut bodies. Ravaged trees, soldiers on the ground wailing under the pain with their torn and charred bodies as if they were burnt with severe fire. The sun slowly showed its oval-face with the fading dark clouds.* The wails of my mother were growing intense, "What have you done, Babru? What you have done is not an ethical act. A mass genocide, Babru. A mass genocide you have committed."

"What are you trying to tell, mother? How would I be held responsible for this massacre? We were retreating after we were attacked with mass numbered poisonous snakes. What are you implying, mother?" I desperately pleaded with my mother to be reasonable with her accusations.

My mother's inconsolable wails suddenly ceased when she saw an orange colour flag with the imprint of a *Lord Hanuman*. She sprinted towards the flag, followed by Manvi and a strange awkward lady with twisted legs.

Gurudeva Lespakamanya too accompanied my mother to the battlefield. I was never bewildered the way I was today. Gurudev never visited a battlefield.

What prompted him to come?

I asked, "Gurudev, what has unfolded that my mother was accusing me of?"

Gurudev gently smiled and rubbed my *Ajna chakra* position between my eyes with his right thumb finger. The veils caging my subconscious memory opened to what had transpired. *The absolute extermination wielded solely by me.* I was overwhelmed with the guilt of total annihilation and at my deplorable actions. Self-immolation seemed to be the only door to repentance. I pulled out the knife attached to my scabbard and when I was about to slash my neck with closed eyes, Gurudev held my hand. Comprehending my turbulent spirit, he pointed me to where mother was sobbing, holding someone's hand.

I staggeringly walked towards my mother, inundated with the flood of guilt. When I moved closer to her, I was astonished to learn the man my mother was grieving for, holding his hand dearly, was that arrogant king, wielder of celestial weapons responsible for wiping out my army. My heart raced at a rapid pace when that arrogant man who was struggling to inhale signalled with his hand for me to approach him.

What should be done? Should I grab my mother and run? Why is my mother showing concern for this stranger? Who is this person?

"Son, I am husband to your mother, Chitrangada and.....hm,......and I am your father, Arjuna Pandava." he ushered in a crumbling tone and continued, "I am very proud of you, son. For you have defeated me, whom even the greatest of warriors failed to achieve."

I slid into total darkness. Total emptiness seized my spirit and mind in its entirety. "Father" "I am your father, Arjuna Pandava" echoed and echoed in the gloomy corners of my mind. The ridiculous laughs of the immodest tormentors hurling "Bastard" at me kept knocking my consciousness again and again. Now, I have this man, my hostile enemy claiming to be my birth father. But, all I had in my mind is the picture of my lone abused woman, my mother, my innocent mother. Should I blame him, for he abandoned us? Should I curse him, for he never cared to at least pay a visit or play with his son?

I extended my hand to hold and caress his hand dearly. Looking into his pain-stricken eyes, I wanted to say, "My name is Babruvahana, your abandoned son," but he collapsed into a lifeless body, lying there breathless, motionless before I could say, "My name is Babruvahana, your abandoned son." Yet, I mumbled, "My name is Babruvahana." I said, "My name is Babruvahana." And I shouted, "My name is Babruvahana." But, his life had already ebbed away.

... ...To be continued

Thank you for your valuable time.
Hope you enjoyed reading it.

Until next time,

Regards,

Characters—

(How well you know the characters)

Kingdom of Manipura				
	Name	**Your answer**		**description**
1	Gurudev Lespakamanya		a	*the leader of Manikuntekans*
2	Rasikri		b	*friend of Gyanvitarna*
3	Durvasana		c	*Horse of Chitrangada*
4	Suprasena		d	*Blacksmith of Manipura*
5	Pinakini		e	*Rathadhyakshas commander-in-chief*
6	Radhasaki		f	*friend of Gyanvitarna*
7	Jubi Chacha		g	*Coin-keeper in tax department of Manipura*
8	Chitrasena		h	*son of Goklevitarna*
9	Ramakhetu and Vishnudar		I	*The Dog*

10	Gyanvitarna		j	The spiritual teacher of Chitrasena, Chitrangada, Babruvahana and Rasikri
11	Goklevitarna		k	The son of Rasikri
12	Bhatukesh		l	grandfather of Babruvahana, father of Chitrangada, king of Manipura
13	Giriraj		m	mother of Babruvahana
14	Chitrangada		n	Minister of Manipura kingdom, instructor of Vedas, father of Gyanvitarna
15	Abhakshi		o	principal advisors to Chitrasena
16	Astabhargava		p	Commander-in-chief of Manipura, trusted aide to Babruvahana
17	Kanteshwara		q	Dear friend of Chitrasena, military strategist and administrator.
18	Manvi		r	Mother of Aitreya
19	Aitreya		s	Head of food department
20	Adi Atulya		t	beloved friend to Babruvahana

-

Kingdom of Kuru				
	Name	Your answer		description
1	Balarama		a	*brother-in-law of Pandavas*
2	Abhimanyu		b	*Rulers of Trigartas*
3	Pradyumna		c	*spiritual teacher of Pandavas*
4	Arjuna		d	*second among the Pandavas*
5	Krishna		e	*first king of Kamyaka*
6	Rukmini		f	*son of Bheem and Draupadi*
7	Subhadra		g	*son of Vasusena*
8	Draupadi		h	*brother of Suyodhana*
9	Sage Vyas		i	*son of Bheem and Hidimbi*
10	Bheem		j	*wife of Bheem and queen of Kamyaka*
11	Hidimb		k	*Wife of Krishna*
12	Hidimbi		l	*Son of Krishna*
13	Sutasoma		m	*Sister of Krishna and Balarama*
14	Suyodhana		n	*mother to Pandavas*
15	Vasusena		o	*eldest of Pandavas*

16	Vrishaketu		p	*fourth among the Pandavas*
17	Dushasana		q	*mammoth elephant of Bhagadatta*
18	Yudhishthira		r	*son of Bhagadatta*
19	Sahadeva		s	*Son of charioteer, dear friend to Suyodhana*
20	Nakula		t	*Brother to Krishna*
21	Ghatotkacha		u	*late king of Pragjyotishpura*
22	Suryavarman, Ketuvarman, Dhritavarman		v	*youngest of Pandavas*
23	Kunti		w	*cousin to Pandavas, contender to Kuru Kingdom*
24	Bhagadatta		x	*third among the Pandavas*
25	Supratika		y	*wife of Pandavas*
26	Vajradatta		z	*Son of Arjuna*

Send the answers by tagging @author11neel in Instagram post. The first hundred to get it right will get goodies from the author.